Report of a Geological Reconnoissance of the State of Indiana

SALZWASSER VERLAG

David Dale Owen

Report of a Geological Reconnoissance of the State of Indiana

Reprint of the original, first published in 1859.

1st Edition 2023 | ISBN: 978-3-37514-210-0

Verlag (Publisher): Salzwasser Verlag GmbH, Zeilweg 44, 60439 Frankfurt, Deutschland
Vertretungsberechtigt (Authorized to represent): E. Roepke, Zeilweg 44, 60439 Frankfurt, Deutschland
Druck (Print): Books on Demand GmbH, In de Tarpen 42, 22848 Norderstedt, Deutschland

REPORT

OF A

GEOLOGICAL RECONNOISSANCE

OF THE

STATE OF INDIANA,

MADE IN THE YEAR 1837,

IN CONFORMITY TO AN ORDER OF THE LEGISLATURE.

BY D. D. OWEN, M. D.,
STATE GEOLOGIST.

PART FIRST.

INDIANAPOLIS:
JOHN C. WALKER, STATE PRINTER.
1859.

PREFATORY REMARKS.

In perusing Geological Reports, the general reader is often at a loss to comprehend much of the matter they contain, as they are couched in language familiar only to those who may have devoted themselves to scientific pursuits. It is doubtless difficult, and in some cases almost impossible to describe scientific facts, without either employing scientific terms, or else entering into long and tedious explanations; yet the most important and practical among geological facts may be generally described in a plain and familiar manner. In this view the present observations on the Geology of Indiana are thrown into as popular and concise a form as possible, and the publication of more detailed scientific facts reserved for some future occasion, when the Geology of the country shall be farther developed.

REPORT.

To the Honorable,

the Legislature of Indiana:

GENTLEMEN—In fulfillment of my duty as Geologist of the State of Indiana, and in accordance with the instructions contained in an act, entitled "An act to provide for a Geological Survey of Indiana," approved February 6, 1837, I have commenced a geological examination of our State, of which I beg to communicate to you the results, in the following

REPORT:

Before entering on the more immediate objects of this report, a few words in reference to the general character and principles of the science of Geology may not be useless nor out of place, and will serve to elucidate the subsequent part of this report.

The science of Geology, of comparatively modern date, is now universally conceded to be one, not of mere curious inquiry, but of vast practical utility. It indicates, not only to the closet philosopher a boundless field of conjecture, whereon to erect theories of creation and systems of the world; but, to the manufacturer, the raw material whence mineral riches are abundantly derived, and to the farmer, the means of improving soils that nature seems to have disfavored.

In older States, and more thickly settled countries,

science, going hand in hand with commercial enterprise, has already seized upon all the mineral riches that more immediately present themselves. Here, in our young State, comparatively untrodden by the footsteps of inquisitive science, we have a rich and productive field on which to imitate their enterprise and rival their discoveries.

Even the imperfect survey which time has yet permitted, has amply established the fact that our citizens often unconsciously tread over hidden stores of mineral riches, which, when the researches of science shall have brought to light, the enterprise of this age of improvement will quickly seize upon, increasing at once the fortunes of individuals and the resources of the State. The entire western portion of Indiana proves, on examination, to be rich in coal; and though our forests, in a measure, supply the place of this mineral, for the time being, the axe is busily at work among them, and the rapid increase of steam power, calling incessantly for fuel, is thinning them out from year to year.

If it be argued, as it frequently is, that the researches of science are usually curious rather than profitable, I reply, first, that this greatly depends, in the case of geology, upon the course pursued by the geologist; and, secondly, that many scientific questions and learned-sounding classifications, which at first sight appear to involve considerations of an abstract nature alone, do, in fact, lead to the solution of most practical and profitable problems.

I have considered it my duty, while surveying a country as new as ours, to remember that a State just settling is like a young man starting in life, whom it behooves to secure to himself a competency before he indulges in unproductive fancies. I have considered it the most important object to search out the hidden resources of the State, and open new fields of enterprise to her citizens. That object effected, time enough will remain to institute inquiries (which a liberal policy forbids us to overlook) of a less productive and more abstract character; inquiries which are interesting in a scientific, rather than a commercial, point of view.

Yet must it be borne in mind, that some of the more abstruse doctrines are essential to the successful prosecution of a search after mineral resources. It might, at first sight, appear that a technical examination of the various geological formations in our State, of their relative superposition and inclination, and of the organic remains they contain, it might seem, to many, I repeat that such examination held out little promise of productive result. Those who would thus decide, are not aware, or must have forgotten, that certain minerals are uniformly found in certain formations — often in one formation only. When, therefore, the character of a formation is known, the geologist can at once decide what minerals are likely to be contained within it, and what other minerals it would be useless to look for there. Thus, the peroxide of tin (tin ore) is never found except in a primary formation; while bog-iron ore occurs in the more recent alluvial and diluvial deposits. It would be equally a waste of time to look for the former amongst fossiliferous rocks, and for the latter in granite or other allied rocks. Instances are numerous of great waste of time and money by those to whom these truths are not familiar. One occurs to me in which the venerable Charles Carroll of Carrollton was, if my memory serve me, a party interested. It happened in Maryland, near Chesapeake Bay. The proprietor of the land chanced to see *lignite* scattered over its surface, and supposing it to be imperfect coal, he and several others sunk a shaft, obtained an experienced practical miner from England, and expended upwards of twenty thousand dollars in anticipation of large profits from a rich coal mine. A scientific gentleman living in the neighborhood, knowing that the formation in which they were at work was one in which coal is not found, endeavored, without success, to dissuade the projectors from their undertaking.

They neglected his remonstrances; and I need hardly add that the search was wholly abortive, and that the expenses incurred proved a dead loss. The above example is the more striking, as the English miner, who came over with the most satisfactory recommendations as a workman of extensive practical experience, positively contracted to find a coal-bed at a certain depth.

Instances might be multiplied, in which appearances have, in a similar manner, deceived the unscientific observer. A black bituminous slate, entirely unfit for fuel, occurs frequently in our State, which is continually mistaken for coal, because it resembles coal-shale, and burns for a short time when thrown on the fire.

Again—sulphuret of iron, of little value, is very frequently picked up as gold and silver ore, on account of its color and metallic appearance. Mica, too, is said to have deceived the avarice of the early settlers of Virginia; the more readily, perhaps, that their imaginations were inflamed by the tales of countless riches amassed by the followers of Cortez and Pizarro in the southern portion of the New World.

Hence the importance of accurate scientific research, and of a general examination of the various geological formations of the State.

But again; the relative ages, and consequently nature and position, of the various members of the stratified formations, is best ascertained, not from the lithological character, (mineral structure of the rock,) but from the occurrence or non-occurrence of the petrified remains of animals and plants, and by the particular nature of these remains. Hence the examination of fossil remains is intimately connected with the discovery of mineral riches.

Those unfamiliar with the science of geology will better appreciate the foregoing, and more easily comprehend the observations contained in the body of the report, by giving their attention to the following brief remarks, containing the

LEADING PRINCIPLES OF GEOLOGY.

Distinctions between stratified and crystalline rocks.

When we examine the crust of our earth, with respect to the external appearance of its rock formations, we discover two marked and distinct classes of rocks; one formed out of rounded stony particles, disposed in layers, and frequently containing the forms of animals or plants, termed fossils or petrifactions, incased in their substance; the other not made up of rounded component particles, but rather of angularcry stals, partaking more or less of regular geometrical forms intruding one upon the other, and never imbedding organic remains. These, in geological language, are termed, the former *stratified* or *aqueous;* the latter *crystalline, igneous* or *primitive* rocks.*

Origin of stratified and crystalline rocks.

The stratified rocks seem to have been deposited from water, at irregular intervals, throughout a long series of ages; while the crystalline, closely resembling productions of the laboratory and workshops, formed by a gradual consolidation from a molten to a solid state, are believed to have had an igneous origin. These two classes of rocks have been respectively divided, for the sake of distinction, into several groups or subdivisions each of which has its own peculiar ores and minerals.

Grouping of the rocks.

Rule for the sub-division of rocks.

The subdivisions of the crystalline rocks depend on differences in their mineral composition, when the lines of demarkation between the subdivisions of the stratified rocks are marked chiefly by decided differences in their imbedded fossils. *This order of succession, in every known portion of our globe, is invariable.* Sometimes, indeed almost always, one or more of the groups is wholly or partially wanting, but their order of succession is *never inverted.* Thus, the first group, if found at all, lies

Order of succession invariable.

---

* Diagrams accompanied the original manuscript, but, as these were not engraved, reference to them is omitted.

universally *above* all the others; the second, above all except the first; and so on to the end. This is the grand principle which guides the geologist in his researches—which enables him to say, "*Here* we may find gold; *here* lead," and which teaches him to predict what layers of rocks must be successively penetrated in boring to any great depth in the earth. But for this all his researches would be in the dark, and his predictions could be at best but shrewd, and often erroneous, conjectures.

First Division.

The *first*, uppermost, and therefore most recent of the subdivisions is called the *alluvium;* it includes all deposits similar to river bottoms, produced by causes now in action, and encloses the remains of animals and plants only of existing species. Of this formation we have extensive examples in our western country, particularly towards the mouths of large rivers.

Second Division.

The *second*, the *Quaternary* epoch, including loose deposits of silicious marl, sand, clay, gravel, both stratified and unstratified drift, osseous breccia (bone beds) and bowlders, (lost or rolled rocks.)

This formation is distinguished from the first, since the deposits of which it is composed have been accumulated at more distant periods and often occupy more elevated situations, and have been formed by causes not immediately apparent, nor now in action. A marked characteristic of this formation is the occurrence in it of the remains of remarkable animals allied to the living sloths but of extinct and often gigantic species; such as the Megalonyx, Megatherium and Mylodon; as well as for the position of erratic blocks, often of enormous size, and occupying situations far removed from the parent rock. Of these we have fine examples in the northern part of Indiana and in the prairies of Iowa.

The rock deposits of this period were accumulated during the *Age of Gigantic Sloths*. There are found also remains of the Mammoth and Mastodon, but since the latter occur also in an underlying formation they are not so *exclusively* characteristic of this period. This is the sub-appennine division of European authors; sometimes called also the Pleistocene Period.*

The *third*, the Tertiary formation, composed chiefly of marine deposits with, locally, some intercalations of fresh-water beds, is distinguished from the two foregoing by containing fossil remains, both of marine and land animals, some of which are of extinct species; the proportion of extinct species increasing as you descend in the formation. Another difference worthy of remark is, that no authentic instances are yet on record of the remains of man, or of his works, having been found in this or any lower formation, these being confined to the most recent deposits. **Third Division.**

The rocks of this period were deposited during the *Age of Gigantic Mammalia.*

The *fourth* great division comprises the Secondary rocks, which embrace a variety of groups from the chalk to the new red sandstone and Permian System inclusive. The ferruginous and green sands of New Jersey, and the chalk marl, or "rotten limestone" of the western district of Tennessee, and the brown stone of the Connecticut valley, may be cited as examples of some of the members of this division, as they exist in our country. Imbedded in these deposits are numerous extinct species of marine and land reptiles, associated with which are numerous fossil, marine shells, of which the one called *Exogyra Costata* is perhaps the most characteristic and abundant in our country. In England this formation is the principal repository of salt; but in the Western States this valuable material appears to be most abundant towards the base of the succeeding group in the descending order. **Fourth Division.**

This formation marks the *Age of Gigantic Reptiles.*

The *fifth* is the bituminous coal formation. Repetitions of beds of sandstone, shale, seams of coal, clays, bands and nodules of iron stone, and occasional beds of **Fifth Division coal formation.**

---

* This is considered by some geologists as the highest and most recent member of the Tertiary System.

limestone compose this group. The strata occupying the upper part of the Cumberland range of mountains, in Kentucky and Tennessee, and those in the western part of this State, may be cited as examples of this group.

This, the independent coal period, may be considered the *Age of the Carboniferous Flora*, and indicates a condition of the earth's surface more favorable for the production of workable beds of coal than any preceding or succeeding period.

The coal-measures rest on what I have designated the sub-carboniferous group, consisting of a series of limestones, with subordinate fine-grained sandstones and shales, such as occur at the base of the Cumberland range of mountains, and in part of Perry, Harrison and Floyd counties, in this State.

Sixth Division

The *sixth* is the black Lingula slate formation, (the Devonian, or Old Red Sandstone of European writers,) such as occurs at the base of the knobs of Floyd county. This black slate is often confounded with and mistaken for coal, as it is sometimes so highly charged with bitumen that it will burn for a short time though it is not reduced to ashes. But it lies, as will be shown, many hundred feet lower in the geological formations than the true, workable coal. The upper coralline limestones and fish beds of the Falls of the Ohio may also be classed in this group.

This may be designated the *Age of Buckler-headed and Enamel-scaled Fishes*.

Seventh Division.

The *seventh* consists, in the Western States, of magnesian limestones more or less pure, characterized principally by remains of corals, with some marine shells and trilobites. These strata pass downwards into shell-limestones, with alternating marlites and fine-textured mudstones, giving rise usually, in the west, to the "Blue Limestone" formation, and prevailing through the "Blue grass" regions both of this State, Kentucky and Tennessee.

Associated with the marine fossil shells and corallines

of this period are abundant remains of crustaceans allied to the horse-shoe crab, which from their three-lobed structure have been called *Trilobites:* hence this period may aptly be denominated the "Age of Trilobites." This is the Silurian formation of European authors.

The shell limestones and marlites repose in the northwest on a quartzose sandstone formation, known under the name of the Potsdam sandstone. This, or at least the lower part of it, is classed by some authors with the Cambrian system of Sedgewick; others contend that it corresponds with the lower members of the Silurian System of Murchison, and is not entitled to be considered as a distinct system by itself. **Potsdam sandstone.**

These comprise the whole of the stratified, sedimentary rocks, at present, known in this country. It ought to be observed, however, that in some of the mountainous districts, as you approach the granite, there are rocks more or less stratified and possessing sometimes a semi-crystalline structure. These are considered to be some of the above stratified rocks, which have been more or less metamorphosed by their proximity to lines of igneous action; *i. e.*, altered by heat: such rocks have been distinguished by some authors under the name of "metamorphic." **Metamorphic rocks.**

In contradistinction to the above enumerated strata, which are, in fact, sediments once deposited at the bottom of the ocean, the unstratified, crystalline rocks, like granite, sienite and greenstone, in which no definable petrified remains of animals have yet been found, form the nucleus or base on which the preceding stratified and metamorphic rocks repose, and which, as will hereafter be more fully detailed, have, not unfrequently, been elevated by subterraneous action into the highest peaks of the mountain ranges. These have been denominated, by some authors, the primitive rocks, because they appear to have been the source whence the particles have been derived, by abrasion, erosion or chemical forces, that accumulated to form this vast pile of sedimentary strata, equal in thickness to many miles.

In the leaves of this gigantic book we not only read the records of the past history of this everchanging planet, but we find also entombed together the fossil fuel and the iron ore, which have contributed, beyond a doubt, more than any other two minerals to the civilization and well-being of man. It is the province of the geologist to develope and make known the localities where these and other valuable mineral riches may be found and worked with profit; and it is the chemist, who, by his analyses in the laboratory, investigates the quality and proportion of the mineral wealth which the labors of the geologist exhume.

Had these strata remained in their original, nearly horizontal, position, we could have known but little of any but the uppermost layers, as the deepest mines have only been penetrated a few thousand feet. It may be perceived, however, that long continued subterranean force, acting from beneath and aided occasionally by paroxysmal throes, might overcome the resistance of the superincumbent mass and finally rend asunder, at weak points, the solid crust of the earth, which, though many miles in thickness, is, nevertheless, quite thin, compared with the whole diameter of our globe; and thus the upper strata might be displaced and worn away by the powerful currents, established in the ocean at periods of extensive volcanic action, and by this means the inferior strata might, by degrees, protrude and become exposed, and the crystalline and inferior stratified rocks would naturally, if the elevating forces continued in action for a sufficient length of time, gradually rise higher and higher, and finally occupy the most elevated positions on the lofty and ragged mountain sides and peaks; while the others would come in regular succession to the surface, flanking the mountain sides and extending over the plains and inferior ridges, so that the newest rocks might occupy the depressed basins or valleys remote from the high mountain ranges, though they were the last deposited. This, at first view, might appear a geological paradox; but when we reflect that the materials, which went to form the most modern rocks, are derived from the wear and decay of mountain masses, and that all fine earthy materials have a constant tendency to be transported by running water into the lowest positions, (first by the mountain rill, into the nearest brook, thence by smaller streams carried into large rivers, which finally disembogue into the sea, carrying in their turbid waters the ruins of a higher country,) we at once perceive the solution of the apparent paradox.

This, in effect, is what actually occurred in this country. Let us suppose a cut along a line from Terre Haute, in the north-west, extending south-east through Kentucky and Tennessee to a point in the Cumberland range of mountains nearer the corner of Georgia and Alabama. Along the valley of the Wabash we find the Quaternary deposits reposing on the coal-measures, which latter formation prevails through western Indiana and Kentucky until we reach the valley of Green river. Here the sub-carboniferous limestone appears rising from beneath the lowest beds of the coal-measures; on the northern confines of Tennessee the black Lingula slate and underlying coralline limestone reach the surface, coming from beneath the sandstones and shales that constitute the base of the sub-carboniferous group. In Middle Tennessee the Blue limestone constitutes the surface rock with the afore-mentioned slates, shales, sandstones and limestones, forming a kind of amphitheatre of hills, encircling and superimposed on the inferior limestones, which are again hidden from view until we reach East Tennessee; these inferior limestones of Silurian date gradually rise toward the Alleghany range and finally blend with the metamorphic and gneissoid rocks that flank the granite nucleus of that range of mountains.

Thus we see each group may come in regular succession to the surface, and those strata, originally most deeply seated, are heaved up into the loftiest peaks of the mountain ranges. It is only by such an arrangement that many of our valuable mineral deposits could have become accessible, since most of the metallic ores are confined to inferior strata. As it is, all the formations are presented to the geologist in different portions of our globe; and since, as before remarked, particular metals are confined to certain groups, highly important practical results are secured by a careful examination of the extent and localities of the various formations; and as a consequent, by the study of the imbedded fossils, the presence of which constitutes the most decisive evidence of the identity of geological strata.

This is a brief sketch of principles, upon which, as a basis, science is now engaged in raising a magnificent superstructure; her efforts will not only bring to light hidden truths respecting the remote history of our earth, but will assuredly facilitate practical investigation, in which are intimately involved our political and commercial welfare.

PLAN OF CONDUCTING THE SURVEY.

Spring and summer survey.

The geological survey, so far as yet conducted, has been of a general character, the object having been chiefly to gain a correct and connected idea of the whole, before spending much time in detailed examinations in any particular spot. With this view, the spring and summer survey was commenced by running a line from the mouth of the Wabash to the south-eastern limit of the State, passing through Posey, Vanderburg, Warrick, Spencer, Perry, Crawford, Harrison, Floyd, Clark, Scott, Jefferson, Switzerland, and Dearborn counties, keeping as close to the meanders of the Ohio river as possible, in order to take advantage of the sections exposed on the bluffs along its banks.

Another line was then run through Ripley county to the town of Madison; from thence, a zig-zag line through Jennings and Bartholomew counties, to Columbus; thence through Jackson, Washington, Orange, Lawrence, and Monroe counties, back to Columbus; thence, through Johnson and Marion counties, to Indianapolis; through Hancock, Rush, Fayette, Union, and Franklin counties, to Brookville; from Brookville, through Decatur and Shelby counties, back to Indianapolis; from Indianapolis again, through the corner of Hendricks and Putnam counties, to Putnamville; from Putnamville to the falls of Eel river and into part of Owen county; thence, through Vigo county to Terre Haute; from Terre Haute, along the meanders of the Wabash, through Sullivan, Knox, Gibson, Pike, and Posey, back to the place of beginning; thus including, in these various lines, all the counties lying south of the National Road, except Greene, Daviess, Martin and Dubois.

In my fall examination, I visited those southern counties which were not included in my spring and summer survey; namely, Greene, Daviess, Martin and Dubois. Fall excursion.

I then proceeded north, with a view of discovering where the lines marking the limits of the formation, crossed the Wabash, and whether they continued on in the same northerly curve in which I had traced them, as far as to the National Road. With this view, I passed through Parke, Montgomery, and the northern part of Fountain county, crossed the Wabash at Attica, and explored the country about Pine creek; re-crossed the Wabash and proceeded along its south-east bank to Lafayette, Americus, Delphi, and Logansport, thence along the Michigan road, to the crossing of the Tippecanoe; thence by Yellow river to Laporte and Michigan City. After making some examinations along Lake Michigan, I went to South Bend, Mishawaka, and a short distance into Elkhart county, intending to reach

Fort Wayne, and return down the Wabash to Logansport; but being detained nearly a week in consequence of an accident, I was compelled to return by the shorter route along the Michigan Road. From Logansport, I passed down the north side of the Wabash to Lafayette, thence along the Wea to Crawfordsville; thence to Spencer and the junction of Eel and White rivers; and returned through Bloomfield, Washington, Petersburgh and Princeton, to New Harmony.

DETAILS OF THE SURVEY.

SUMMER SURVEY.

(SOUTH OF THE NATIONAL ROAD.)

Although, in many situations, it has been difficult to obtain a view of the actual rock formations, on account of the many deep and extensive alluvial and drift deposits which have overspread and covered these sometimes to a great depth; yet sufficient was disclosed to determine satisfactorily the succession of the formations, and to point out the general course of the lines which mark their limits. In many cases, too, I had an opportunity of observing the characteristic fossils peculiar to the different strata, and of fully proving the fact, that the order of superposition is identical with that witnessed in many other distant parts of this western country; also, that the characteristic fossils of each series of strata coincide, in a very striking manner, with those found in the corresponding strata throughout these western States.

Dip of the strata.

Satisfactory proof has also been obtained that the strata do not lie perfectly horizontal, although they may appear to do so when viewed over a small extent of country only; but that there is a slight general dip of the strata towards the west, or west and south is unquestionable;* and not unfrequently they assume an undulatory direction. The whole strata, therefore, gent-

---

* Locally the dip deviates sometimes to the north-west.

ly lean and roll towards the Alleghany range. Hence it is, that, as we travel up stream towards the east, we successively reach older or inferior strata. Hence it is, also, that (if we leave out of view the modern and drift deposits,) the newest formation of Indiana—the coal formation*—is to be found in the western portion of the State.

The first line run showed the following *succession of formations in the counties bordering on the Ohio river.*

Coal formation on the Ohio river.

Along the Ohio river we find the coal formation, taken in the previously defined sense, prevailing through the counties of Posey, Vanderburg, Warrick, Spencer and Perry. At Oil creek, in Perry county, there appears, above the drainage of the country, a bed of limestone. From this point the coal-measures only occupy the ridges; the limestone, though subject to occasional undulations, gradually rises higher and higher into the ridges, and finally, near the confines of Harrison county, extends to their most elevated summits.

Sub-carboniferous limestone on the Ohio river.

The beds of limestone, above referred to on Oil creek, are the upper members of this great limestone group which extends, in Harrison county, from the lowest positions visible to the summit levels of the country. To this calcareous group I have applied the name sub-carboniferous, as indicating its position beneath the true coal-measures, since in no instance, as yet, have any *workable* beds of coal been found associated with these limestones; and here I may cite, not only the practical importance of the principles of geology, but also the value of the palaeontological tests applied to determine the position of coal; undoubtedly one of the most valuable of all minerals.

Archimedes and Pentremital limestones.

The upper beds of the above limestone group contain certain fossils, only two of which I will particularly call attention to here; the *Archimedes* of Lesueur, and the

* It is important here to remark, that, by *coal formations*, is meant, not merely seams of coal, but a region in which coal occurs, associated, as it always is, with beds of sandstone, shale, clay and limestone.

Pentremites globosa of Goldfuss. From the time of my first acquaintance with Western Geology I have diligently and closely observed the geological horizon of these two petrifactions; not in one single instance have I, yet, discovered a *workable* coal *beneath* the limestones forming the matrix of these organic remains. One or two thin beds of coal there are below this geological level; but not at any locality have I seen a good *workable coal;* and I am convinced that in this part of the Western Continent, at least, the conditions favorable for the formation of coal did not begin to exist until after the deposition of the Archimedes and Pentremital limestones of the upper part of the sub-carboniferous group; and after the extinction of these species of corals and crinoidea. The value and importance of this test, in surveying a country geologically for coal, cannot be overrated, and so far as my present experience goes, it may be regarded as an axiom in Western Geology, that the *productive* coal-measures are confined to rocks more recent and higher in the series than the above mentioned limestones. In the southern belt of its range through Indiana, this group has numerous alternations of sandstones in its upper part, and it passes downward into fine-grained freestones, with subordinate beds of grey shales, to which the name of Knob-stones may be appropriately applied, since these silicious strata weather into peculiar conical knobs or hills of which I shall speak hereafter. As well to facilitate description as to give precision to the economical geology of the State, it will be useful to observe certain sub-divisions of this sub-carboniferous group. Those which I shall enumerate at present are:

One or two thin beds of coal under Archimedes limestone.

First. The Archimedes and Pentremital limestones, including the oölitic limestones.* This group affords

First sub-division of sub-carboniferous group.

---

* The oolitic limestones have received this name on account of the rock being made up of small egg-shaped grains like the roe of a fish. These limestones must not be confounded with the oolite formation of European authors, which is a group of the secondary rocks prevalent in the Jura Mountains.

some good building materials. From the oölitic members a very white and pure lime is produced, which is much esteemed, and commands a higher price in the market than any other lime burnt on the Ohio river. The oölitic limestones are also capable of receiving a polish, and make a beautiful cream-colored marble. Thin seams and segregations of a silicious material occur in some of the beds, of the nature of chert; sometimes approximating to chalcedony. These being harder, and resisting decomposition longer than the imbedding limestone, are often found strewed on the surface, having fallen out from the disintegrated matrix.

Productal limestones.

Associated with the Pentremital and Archimedes limestones are beds rich in *Producti* fossil shells remarkable for the size and convexity of the dorsal valve which is often provided with long and slender spines. These Productal beds are well developed in the hills above Leavenworth, in Crawford county. It will be interesting and practically useful to ascertain, by analysis, whether this shell limestone contains much phosphoric acid, as is usually the case in calcareous rocks, charged with fossil shells; since, in that case, it will be particularly valuable as a mineral manure applied to land, either in the ground state or burnt to lime.

Thickness of beds.

The entire thickness of these beds, including the intercalated beds of sandstone and marly shales, is some two to three hundred feet. This sub-division prevails from Oil creek to near Indian creek, and forms the upper part of the hills back of Leavenworth, capped in some places with sandstone.

Barren limestone.

Second, The Barren limestones, so denominated because they prevail through the "Barrens" of Harrison, Orange and Lawrence counties. The limestones of this group are mostly close-textured, with frequent alternations of a silicious, cherty material, either compact or assuming the form of burr-stone of white or reddish tints; as east of Corydon, and between Orleans and Lost river. In the middle part horn-stone and chert-layers are quite abundant. It is where these layers reach the surface that the stunted growth of black jack oak grows, so characteristic of the "Barrens." Though the ground is often much encumbered with blocks of this silicious rock the soil itself is by no means barren; on the contrary, especially where the red under-clays prevail, it is excellent for the growth of most kinds of grain. It is probable that this group, besides affording good building material, may contain some good lithographic stones; if quarries were fairly opened in favorable positions, not only in Harrison county, but at other localities along the northern belt of its extension through Washington, Orange, Lawrence and other counties, where it forms the surface rock.

Silicious blocks in the Barrens.

Lithographic limestones.

The most abundant, and perhaps characteristic fossil of these strata, is a reticulated coralline closely allied to the *Gorgonia infundibuliformis* of Goldfuss; it is especially abundant in burr-stone chert-layers in Harrison county.

The cement of this burr-stone chert has usually too little tenacity to render it useful for mill-stones.

Burr mill-stone.

Third. From beneath the lowest of the preceding sub-division, there emerges, in Floyd county, fine textured freestone, very different from the coarse grit-stones of the coal-measures, passing downwards into grey, argillaceous shales. This is the so-called knob-stone or sub-carboniferous sandstone. It forms the knobs of Floyd county, extending, in a northerly course, through the western part of Washington county into Jackson county.

Knob-stones.

On account of the softness of this rock, and ease with which it can be quarried and chiseled, it has often been employed as a building material, but unfortunately frequently proves of little durability, as many of the public works of Indiana testify. Nevertheless, it should be remarked, in regard to this freestone, that, by a proper selection, it not only forms a beautiful material for ornamental architecture, but even a durable building stone. It is only however the whiter and most silicious varieties that dare be used by the builder who constructs ex-

Building stone.

pensive structures. Many of the most elegant fronts in Cincinnati are built of a rock from the equivalent formation, quarried along the Scioto valley and in Lewis county, Kentucky. This rock cuts with great facility into elaborate ornaments, and the very best quality is said even to harden by exposure. But it is only the most experienced stone masons who should be trusted in the selection of building stones from this formation. The argillaceous and ferruginous varieties are worse than useless, as they crumble to pieces in a few years to the mortification and disaster of the householder.

Encrinital limestones.

Interstratified with the knob-stones are a few beds of limestone, which are pre-eminently encrinital, since they are remarkably rich in remains of crinoidea. Some of the beds of this encrinital limestone make good and durable building stones; they are also well suited for the want of the agriculturist. The stiff tenacious clay soils in the valleys between the knobs, formed from the disintegrations of the argillaceous shale, near their base, would be greatly improved by an application of these limestones as a mineral manure which lies in a convevient position in the hills above.

Black bituminous, aluminous slate.

Situation of the black bituminous aluminous slate on Ohio river.

Black bituminous aluminous slate taken for coal.

At the base of this series there occurs an important stratum—the *black bituminous aluminous slate*—which is to be seen, when the water is low, at the New Albany Ferry-Boat landing; also, in Silver creek, between New Albany and Jeffersonville, and thrown out of the excavation of the canal at Louisville. I call it an important stratum, because this black bituminous aluminous slate resembles, both in its external appearance and chemical composition, the coal shale; and since it takes fire and burns for some time, owing to the presence of bitumen and sulphuret of iron, it is frequently mistaken for indications of coal, and even for coal itself.

This same stratum I have seen in a variety of situations; as in the base of the Harpeth ridge and Paradise hills, ten or twelve miles from Nashville; in the Cany Fork ridge, near the western declivity of the Cumberland mountain. In no instance have I ever found it associated with perfect seams of coal; and I have but little hesitation in asserting, that no true coal will ever be found associated with it in our section of country. This inference is the more important, since labor and capital have already been expended, even in our new State, in boring and digging for coal beneath this stratum, and, of course, without possibility of successful result, as far as my observation extends. It differs, too, from the coal-shale, in containing few or no vegetable impressions. Some of the layers contain small Lingulae and Orbiculae.

Boring for coal beneath the bituminous aluminous strata, always unsuccessful.

Under the black slate, and interposed between beds of crinoidal and coralline limestones, is a valuable bed of hydraulic limestone; it is variable in thickness, from a few feet to ten or twelve feet.

The coralline and crinoidal beds, above and below the hydraulic limestone, as exposed on the Falls of the Ohio on the Indiana shore, present perhaps the finest example of the remains of a petrified coral reef, that is to be found in this country. These beds afford an assemblage of the most beautiful fossil corals, amongst which the *Favosites basaltica*, *F. spongites*, *F. maxima*, *F. cornigera*, *Zaphrentes gigantea*, *cystiphyllum* and *Astrea pentagonus*, of Goldfuss, are the most conspicuous.

Coral limestone of the Falls.

Associated with these in the fish-beds are remains of fossil fishes, allied to the *Pterichthis* and *Coccosteus*, but probably of new genera of winged fossil-fishes.

Fish-beds.

These calcareous masses, and perhaps also the overlying black slate, are, therefore, referable to the Devonian period of European authors, i. e., they were deposited during the age of buckler-headed and enameled-scaled fishes, and belong between the sub-carboniferous group and the Magnesian and blue limestone of the Silurian period.

Limestones, that may be referred to the upper part of this system, just appear at the lowest stage of water of the Ohio river, at the principal axis of elevation of the strata on the Falls of the Ohio, and, rising higher and higher, in a north-easterly course, form the surface rock

Magnesian limestone.

in the eastern part of Clarke and Scott counties, and present a bold section on the Ohio river at Charleston Landing.

Magnesian limestone good building stone.

Magnesia enters largely into the composition of the calcareous rocks of the upper members of this group: in fact, some of the beds will probably be found to be true Magnesian limestones, the carbonate of lime and carbonate of Magnesia being nearly in the proportion of their chemical equivalents; when this is the case they make the most durable building materials that can be obtained, and, such rocks usually appearing of a fine buff color, elegant as well as durable structures can be built of them. They are harder to work, however, than the knob freestones, and not so easily got out in good rectangular blocks, therefore not so much sought after by the mason, who always prefers, if he can find it, a freely working rock. Some of the most ancient structures in England, that have resisted the vicissitudes of centuries and are still extant, have been built of true Magnesian limestone, and the most experienced geologists and architects of England, appointed to select a building stone for the new House of Parliament, gave the preference to Magnesian limestone above all other varieties of excellent building materials, which could be found in Great Britain.

Hard to work.

Rocks of Clarke county.

The middle and eastern part of Clarke county is underlaid by these Magnesian limestones, capped in the higher situations with the coralline limestones of the Falls of the Ohio; and these rocks extend, with a northerly course, forming a belt occupying a part of Scott, Jennings and Bartholomew counties.

The Magnesian limestones become more argillaceous towards their base, and contain more oxide of iron, which imparts to them green and pink tints, often disposed in alternating bands, as in some of the quarries towards the tops of the hills, in the southern part of Jefferson county. These banded argillo-Magnesian limestones are by no means a safe material to select for building purposes. The pure buff, overlying Magne-

Banded rock inferior building stones.

sian limestones should always be preferred. Some of the banded beds are also impregnated with bitumen and sulphuret of iron, which causes them to emit a fetid odor when struck with a hammer. Such beds are still more objectionable as building stones.

Many of the rocks of this group have been used as building materials along the line of the Madison and Indianapolis Railroad.

Associated with these, at the forks of the Muscatatuk river, near Vernon and on Big Sandy creek, about eight miles from that place, is a good variety of burr-stone. It is almost entirely made up of remains of fossil corallines, cemented by a siliceous cement, with perhaps, locally, some calcareous matter also. When free from carbonate of lime, this porous, siliceous material affords a good mill-stone; some of our western mills have been supplied with this burr-stone, which makes a pretty good substitute for the French burr; it requires, however, to be more frequently dressed, because the cement is not so tough. **Burr mill-stones.**

Between these Magnesian limestones, more or less impure, and the true "blue limestone" and marlites of Lower Silurian date, some dark grey calcareous layers intervene, some of which possess hydraulic properties. **Hydraulic layers.**

The "blue limestone," proper with its associate beds of marlites and mudstone, is the lowest geological formation visible in Indiana, that I have yet observed. These strata belong to the same date as the Lower Silurian rocks of European authors and the *age of trilobites*, as set forth in a former part of this report. They prevail in the eastern counties of Indiana, bordering on the State of Ohio, and constitute the chief surface formation in the counties of Switzerland, Dearborn, Franklin, Union and Fayette, and form, also, the lower sections of the hills in the greater part of Jefferson, Ripley, Decatur and Rush counties, capped, however, in the western part of these counties, by the banded and other Magnesian limestones, which belong to the superior division of the same system. **Blue limestone formation.**

Upper division. The uppermost members of the lower division of this system are well exposed in the deep cut of the inclined plane on the Madison Railroad. The rock there is of an intermediate character between a limestone and marlite, sometimes called "hard pan," and has enclosed in it large spherical masses of a coral, (*Favistella stellata*,) and crystallizations of pearlspar. There are also imbedded in it fossil bivalve shells, (*Modiolopsis modiolaris.*) This bed is about thirteen feet in thickness.

Marlite. Under the Favistella bed are layers of fossiliferous blue limestones, alternating with marlites for forty or fifty feet, containing *Ambonychia radiata*, *A. carinata*, *Avicula demissa*, *Atrypa increbescens*, together with a variety of other fossils.

Beneath this, about fifteen miles below Madison, in Jefferson county, are some ten to twenty feet of dark grey marlites, under which is a peculiar shell marble of some interest and economical value.

Its geological position is well shown by a section made at the Dean quarry, Marble Hill:

Marble limestone.

1.	Upper cliff, composed chiefly of Magnesian limestones, terminated, at their base, by the "four-foot bed," used in the construction of the court-house at Louisville	93 feet.
2.	Dark grey Madison water limestone	13 feet.
3.	Thin beds of blue limestone, alternating with dark marlite	40 feet.
4.	Dark grey marlite, ("hard pan,")	10 feet.
5.	Ditto, rather darker colored and more indurated	10 feet.
6.	Shell marble, of Dean's quarry, Marble Hill	20 feet.
7.	Alternations of blue limestone and marls	177 feet.
	Total hight of ridge	360 feet.

No. 6 of this section is the marble rock in question, which lies therefore seventy-three feet below the "four-foot bed," used in the construction of the Louisville court-house.

ITS LITHOLOGICAL CHARACTER.

The ordinary beds of blue limestone seldom exceed one foot in thickness, and are usually only from four to eight inches; whereas the united thickness of this bed of shell limestone of Dean's quarry attains a thickness of over twenty feet, with very little or no interstratified marly clay.

It is a purer material than the blue limestone generally, as will be hereafter shown by the chemical analyses; and this arises from the peculiar local circumstances under which the beds, composing this quarry, have been formed.

It is free from these alternations of earthy, marly deposits, which have more or less contaminated and impregnated the *thin* beds of blue limestone, with which they are elsewhere in contact.

It is susceptible of a higher polish; and the polished surface presents a more beautiful and variegated appearance, than the beds of limestone of other localities in the valley of the Ohio.

It is also freer from imperfections and flaws.

Finally, it is more durable.

From the peculiar local circumstances, under which the Marble Hill Rock has been formed, arise the above variations and deviations from the ordinary character and composition of the prevalent beds of the blue limestone formation to which it properly belongs, and which render it a much more suitable material for ornamental purposes and a more valuable building stone.

The greater part of the bed composing the Marble Hill quarry consists of an immense accumulation of spiral marine univalves, belonging to the fossil genus *Murchisonia*, and chiefly to the species *bellacincta*—intermixed with some *bicincta*. These shells are seldom perfect—more frequently broken—the fragments being cemented with calcspar, with occasionally a small per centage of protoxide of iron.

It is pre-eminently a "shell limestone," and has, therefore, not inappropriately been designated by the Messrs. Dean, a "*conchytic marble*," since it combines all the properties received as the technical division of a marble: a limestone capable of receiving a good polish, and presenting a variegated or uniform aspect, agreeable to the eye.

ITS RANGE AND EXTENT.

This shell marble is confined, on the Indiana side of the Ohio river, as far as has yet been ascertained, to about two and a half miles up and down the river, and four miles back in the interior of Jefferson county.

At the lower opening of Dean's quarry it is six feet thick, and at the "comb," or crown, twenty-four feet; and at the upper opening, twenty feet. Beyond the upper openings is a ravine, on the opposite side of which it is not recognizable as a bed distinct from the ordinary layers of blue limestone.

ITS ORIGIN.

The circumscribed area and abrupt termination at the upper ravine is to be accounted for by a local accumulation of the above species of marine shells, which have been drifted into a heap on the margin of a submarine declivity, either by the action of strong currents or waves, which had sufficient velocity to keep suspended, and carry to a more distant position, the finer earthy particles, that form the marly deposits, alternating with the thinner beds of blue limestone; but permitting the broken shells to subside and collect at this particular locality. These were subsequently cemented by the percolation of calcareous waters, forming calcareous spar, which filled the interstices, and firmly cemented the fragments of shells, which, meanwhile, underwent the change that converted them into a fossil condition; the whole constituting a shell limestone of great purity.

The beds in their present condition lie in a succession of step-like receding beds, nearly horizontal, with only a slight rise of the strata down stream, towards the south, at the rate of about five feet in four hundred yards, and contrary to the general prevalent dip, which is towards the south and west.

The various beds of No. 6 of the section repose upon one another in this manner:

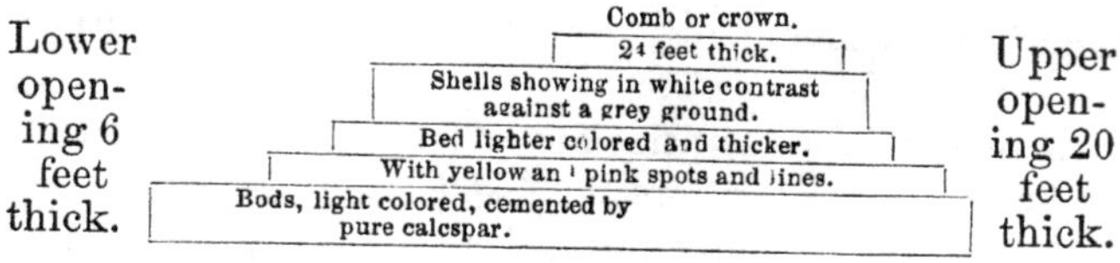

The purest marble lies toward the lower part of the quarry, containing only from 4-10 to 6-10 of one per cent. of insoluble earthy matter. This rock, by reason of the whiteness of the shells and the purity of the cementing calcspar, presents on the "*drove surface*" a cream white, only by a shade darker than statuary marble. When polished, the shells appear white, with light shades of yellow and pink, contrasted upon a warm grey ground, which gives the marble a darker appearance than the "drove surface." At the upper opening the white filling of the shell is frequently surrounded by a zone of pink, the matrix being reddish grey; and one of the uppermost layers of this part of the quarry contains bivalves of considerable size, viz: *Ambonychiæ*, converted into calcspar. This layer affords marble of larger figures, but otherwise similar in colors.

It is only a few inches of the uppermost layers that have received the usual impregnations of the ordinary blue limestone.

The most massive beds lie at the base, near the comb or crown of the deposit, where the beds are 2½ to 3½ or 4 feet thick, with sometimes a close, interlocked suture midway, where, however, the rock is not disposed to part, and which is only indistinctly visible. At the lower opening, the best layers, toward the bottom of the quarry, are from 2 to 3 feet. The Marble Hill quarry is, therefore, capable of affording dimension stones of almost any required size.

ITS ACCESSIBILITY.

The slope of Marble Hill extends immediately down to the margin of the Ohio river; the rock is, therefore, remarkably conveniently situated for shipment either up or down the river.

At present, the facilities for quarrying are greatest at the lower opening, where the "*stripping*" is least; but, when the "comb" opening is fairly entered, the advantages will, undoubtedly, be greatest there, on account of the greater development of the formation, the increased thickness and greater purity of the interior beds; and it is probably here where the best material for ornamental purposes will ultimately be obtained, as well as the largest dimension stones. At this point, the quarry can be wrought without removing any great amount of waste material, as the cliff, of magnesian limestone, (No. 1 of the section,) recedes 100 feet from the mural face of the beds, exposing No. 6 of the section: the intermediate hydraulic and earthy beds having crumbled away, now form a grassy slope.

ITS PHYSICAL CHARACTER.

I have submitted the shell marble to various physical and chemical tests, along with white statuary marble, and eleven other western and eastern building stones, the better to contrast its powers of resisting atmospheric vicissitudes, as compared with other materials now in use in this country. These are numbered for the sake of convenient reference as follows:

No. 1. White Italian Statuary Marble.
" 2. Marble Hill Rock, Jefferson county, Indiana.
" 3. Limestone from the Knobs of Floyd county, Indiana.
" 4. Limestone from White R., Indiana.
" 5. Seneca Freestone, Maryland.
" 6. Little Falls Freestone, New Jersey.

No. 7. Ordinary Blue Limestone, Cincinnati, Ohio.
" 8. A Carboniferous Limestone, Brandenburg, Ky.
" 9. Fine Grained Freestone, Sciota Valley, Ohio.
" 10. Carboniferous Sandstone, Perry county, Indiana.
" 11. Buff-fine Grained Magnesian Limestone, Scott county, Iowa.
" 12. Banded "*four-foot*" Earthy Magnesian Limestone, (Court House Building Stone,) Madison, Indiana.

In the subsequent descriptions of the physical and chemical characters of the above rocks, they will be referred to according to the above appended numbers.

Samples of all the above rocks, were selected, measuring about 1¼ inches long, 1 inch wide, and about ¼ of an inch thick, and made nearly of equal weights, viz: 13.5 French grammes.

The exact specific gravity of each was first taken to ascertain their respective densities or compactness and degree of porosity, which would indicate, to a certain extent, their susceptibility of imbibing water.

Their specific gravity or weight, compared with water as unity, resulted as follows:

No. 1.	No. 2.	No. 3.	No. 4.	No. 5.	No. 6.	No. 7.	No. 8.	No. 9.	No. 10.	No. 11.	No. 12.
2.711	2.683	2.636	2.510	2.507	2.423	2.680	2.556	2.356	2.380	2.515	2.660

Next to the white Italian marble, therefore, the Marble Hill stone has the closest texture of the above 12 varieties of rock; and we may infer from this that, all other things being equal, it would imbibe less water than any of those below it, in the scale of specific gravity. Let us see how this agrees with actual experiment, to test this property in particular.

After exposure for a week to a dry atmosphere, in a room with a stove, these various specimens were accurately weighed on a delicate chemical balance, turning with the thousandth part of a gramme.* They were then soaked in water for ten minutes, taken out, pressed

* A French gramme is equal to 15,444 grains.

between folds of blotting paper, until they no longer left a wet spot, and reweighed.

They were then found to have imbibed water as follows, in decimals of grammes and grammes:

No. 1.	No. 2.	No. 3.	No. 4.	No. 5.	No. 6.	No. 7.	No. 8.	No. 9.	No. 10.	No. 11.	No. 12.
0.028	0.018	0.314	0.410	1.130	1.395	0.047	0.215	0.540	0.621	0.960	0.274

The Marble Hill stone No. 2 has, therefore, less disposition to drink up water than any stone on the list, statuary marble not excepted. This is one very essential property in favor of its durability.

Another proof of its little disposition to imbibe water is found in the fact, that, in very damp weather, the moisture condenses in globules on the surface of No. 2, the Marble Hill stone, while, with the same degree of moisture, No. 3, the Knob-stone, and No. 4, the White River stone, drink the moisture into their pores, and become of a darker color in consequence.

By comparing the specific gravities and amounts of imbibed water, it will be seen that, though there is considerable correspondence, viz: that the lowest in the scale of specific gravity imbibe the most; yet, there is some deviation, which arises from differences in the densities of the particles of which the rock is made up, and perhaps also from differences in the chemical composition.

To ascertain the rate of drying, these various specimens were now exposed to a dry atmosphere, in a room heated by a stove, and weighed after the lapse of one hour. They retained water as follows:

No. 1.	No. 2.	No. 3.	No. 4.	No. 5.	No. 6.	No. 7.	No. 8.	No. 9.	No. 10.	No. 11.	No. 12.
0.005	0.011	0.059	0.250	0.463	0.400	0.070	0.084	0.383	0.470	0.805	0.259

They were again weighed after three hours, and still retained water as follows:

No. 1.	No. 2.	No. 3.	No. 4.	No. 5.	No. 6.	No. 7.	No. 8.	No. 9.	No. 10.	No. 11.	No. 12.
0.004	0.005	0.024	0.120	0.284	0.285	0.011	0.052	0.082	0.243	0.598	0.140

In less than four hours No. 1 and No. 2 had lost all their water. In 4½ hours, No. 7 and 8 had lost all their water; while No. 3 took six hours, and No. 4 still retained, at the end of six hours, 0.013 of water. The freestones No. 5 and No. 6 were hardly dry after eighteen hours exposure.

As it is the freezing of imbibed water, that is chiefly instrumental in scaling rocks during frosts, the above experiments give us, to some extent, an insight into the durability of these materials; those that imbibe least water, as a general rule, being least liable to be scaled; but, as this property depends also upon the cohesive and chemical forces which hold the particles together, we cannot, from these tests *alone*, pronounce on the durability of a rock.

In order to supply what is considered by French architects the best criterion by which to judge of the action of frost upon rocks, I submitted all the above specimens to the efflorescing or crystallizing action of sulphate of soda in the manner proposed by M. Brard.

But before I proceeded to this investigation, all the specimens, when quite dry, were again weighed, to ascertain how much they had lost by submersion and abrasion, while passing through the previous processes.

The various specimens had lost weight as follows:

No. 1.	No. 2.	No. 3.	No. 4.	No. 5.	No. 6.	No. 7.	No. 8.	No. 9.	No. 10.	No. 11.	No. 12.
0.004	0.004	0.009	0.017	0.001	0.015	0.011	0.037	0.007	0.013	0.013	0.016

This gives the relative amount of loss which each suffers by alternate wet and dry, and by wear and tear.

The Seneca freestone stands at the head of the list in this experiment; next follows the Italian marble and Marble Hill rock, both of which lost the same amount. The Knob stone lost more than twice as much; the Blue Limestone nearly three times as much; and the White River stone more than four times as much.

THE ACTION OF SULPHATE OF SODA.

All the rocks were now immersed in a boiling-hot solution of Sulphate of Soda, saturated in the *cold*, and kept there for thirty minutes. They were then suspended by horsehairs, previously wound round them, from a frame work over cups containing a portion of the same solution. When the water had so far evaporated as to exhibit the saline particles, appearing as an efflorescence on the surface of the specimens, (viz: next morning,) they were all simultaneously dipped into the solution of sulphate of soda contained in the cup provided for each; left there for fifteen minutes; and then raised out, so as to be suspended, each over its respective cup as before; so that all particles scaled off from each specimen were received into its appropriate cup. This process was continued for three days; the rocks, during that period, having been immersed three times in the saline solution in the cups, independent of the first submersion in the hot solution. At the end of that time the scaled particles were collected, washed, dried, ignited and weighed. The disintegrated particles weighed as follows:

No. 1.	No. 2,	No. 3.	No. 4.	No. 5.	No. 6.	No. 7.	No. 8.	No. 9.	No. 10.	No. 11.	No. 12.
0.014	0.009	0.030	0.018	0.017	0.011	0.029	0.023	0.052	0.148	0.010	0.088

The Marble Hill rock No. 2 lost by these three days action of the sulphate of soda less than any one on the list, the Italian marble not excepted. Next to it the fine grained magnesian limestone No. 11 withstood the action best.

The process of immersion in the cold solution contained in the cups, and suspension for efflorescence in the air over them, was renewed and continued for three days more. After the lapse of that time the disintegrated particles were collected as before, washed, dried, ignited, and weighed as follows:

No. 1.	No. 2.	No. 3.	No. 4.	No. 5.	No. 6.	No. 7.	No. 8.	No. 9.	No. 10.	No. 11.	No. 12.
0.014	0.029	0.050	0.100	0.070	0.073	0.086	0.030	0.139	0.426	0.080	0.280

In these last three days the amounts scaled off were greater than in the first three days, as the action goes on in an increasing ratio by reason of the surface becoming broken up.

In this experiment the Italian marble suffered least loss, but next to it the Marble Hill rock withstood the further disintegrating action best.

I should have exposed other specimens to the direct

action of frost itself after being soaked in water, but the weather was not sufficiently cold.

The process of saline efflorescence or crystallization, as followed above, gives, however, a very good approximation towards the powers of resistance of limestone rocks, though I am disposed to think that it acts relatively more upon sandstone, and is, therefore, a better criterion to judge of the relative durability of limestones amongst themselves, than of limestones as compared with sandstones.

CHEMICAL EXAMINATION.

The next step in my researches into the properties of the Marble Hill rock was its chemical analysis: For this purpose I selected two varieties, one taken from near the base of the lower opening, (No. 2*a*,) and one from the upper opening, with spots and lines of light yellow in the interstices between the shells, *Murchisonia bellacincta*, and *bicincta*, (No. 2*b*.)

	No. 2*a*.	No. 2*b*.
Moisture	0.001	gramm. 0.001
Lime	0.460	0.505
Magnesia	0.050	0.018
Protoxide of Iron	0.0328	0.015
Alumina	0.0052	0.010
Insoluble Earthy Matter	0.002	0.020
Carbonic Acid	0.434	0.426
Phosphoric Acid	0.006	0.005
Manganese	*a trace.*	*a trace.*
Loss and Alkalies	0.010	....
	1.000	1.000

These constituents appear to be combined in the rock as follows:

	No. 2*a*.	No. 2*b*.
Carbonate of Lime	81.6	89.68
Carbonate of Magnesia	10.5	3.80

	No. 2*a*.	No. 2*b*.
Carb. of the Protoxide of Iron....	5.28	2.30
Phosphate of Lime..................	0.90	0.85
Alumina	0.52	1.00
Insoluble Earthy Matter	0.20	2.00
Moisture	0.10	0.10
Manganese	*trace.*	*trace.*
Loss and Alkalies	0.90	0.21
	100.00	100.00

I now place these in contrast with the analyses of five others of the above limestone.

	No. 1.	No. 2.	No. 4.	No. 7.	No. 12
Moisture		00.3	00.1	00.3	00.4
Insoluble earthy matter,	00.10	2.9	1.9	1.3	29.0
Lime.......................	55.50	51.0	53.96	53.58	24.64
Magnesia.................	00.54	00.9	00.72	00.50	10.97
Alumina and Iron	00.35	01.9	00.40	01.80	03.20
Carbonic Acid...........	43.00	42.0	42.79	42.30	31.00
Phosphoric Acid.........		*trace.*		00.12	
Sulphuric Acid..........					00.13
Chlorine...................					*trace.*
Manganese	*slight tr.*	*trace*	*slight tr.*		
Loss and Alkalies.......	.51	1.10	.13	00.10	00.66
	100.00	100.0	100.00	100.00	100.00

No. 12. The four foot bed, variegated with reddish, greenish and buff bands, is an impure, earthy, magnesian limestone of variable composition, as will be seen by two other analyses of the same rock:

Moisture	00.4	00.4
Insoluble Earthy matter................	25.0	18.5
Lime	28.0	30.0
Magnesia	10.06	14.7
Alumina and Iron........................	3.40	3.4

Carbonic Acid	32.00	32.4
Sulphuric Acid	0.13	0.12
Chlorine	*trace.*	*trace.*
Loss and Alkalies	1.01	00.47
	100.00	100.00

From observing a considerable analogy between the proportion of the chemical constituents of this "*four foot bed*" and the Rondout hydraulic limestone extensively used in the State of New York, for the purposes of hydraulic cement, I was induced to burn some of it, grind it, and mix it with a certain amount of sand and water to the consistence of a mortar, to see whether it would set under water. The day after it was made up it was already quite firm and not at all disposed to soften under water. Thus it appears that the court house of Louisville has actually been constructed of a limestone possessing hydraulic properties—rocks which are remarkable for the facility with which they split, scale and crumble by exposure to the weather.

A fine grained, magnesian limestone, similar to No. 11 from Quarry Creek, Scott county, Iowa, yielded by analysis the following ingredients:

Carbonate of Lime	52.15
Carbonate of Magnesia	42.10
Oxide of Iron and Alumina, dissolved by acid,	1.90
Insoluble Earthy Matter	1.20
Moisture	1.55
Loss	1.1
	100.00

Magnesian limestone, in which the carbonate of lime and carbonate of magnesia are nearly in the proportion of their chemical equivalents, with but three to five per cent. of insoluble earthy matter, are acted on quite differently by atmospheric agencies compared with the effect produced on No. 12; indeed, experience has generally proved them to be durable rocks, and it will be seen that one of them, No. 11, withstood the action of sulphate of soda, during the first three days well—next best to the Marble Hill stone, losing only 0.010, while No. 12 lost 0.088—nearly nine times as much.

The impurities in a limestone may be regarded as the insoluble earthy material, and the alumina dissolved in part by the acid. The specimen No. 2*a* analyzed indicated only seven-tenths of one per cent. of these earthy ingredients. The Knob stone contains nearly five per cent. of these ingredients; and the White river stone two and a half per cent. The White river stone is a purer limestone than the Knob stone, but it is more cellular and has more imperfection of surface, and hence imbibes four times as much water as the Knob stone, and twenty-two times as much as the Marble Hill rock.

The ordinary blue limestone has over three per cent. of earthy impurities, and imbibes seven times as much water as the Marble Hill rock.

The above examinations supply abundant evidence of the durability, purity and excellence of the Marble Hill rock. But any one who will take the trouble to visit the quarry and examine the rock in place, can obtain additional proof, if he desires it, of these facts.

He can there see blocks, which were quarried in December during times of alternate freezing and thawing, and which have been lying exposed for four years, which still retain all their original sharpness of edge, and without any appearance of cracks or stains. He will, moreover, perceive that the various layers composing this formation, (No. 6 of this section,) present themselves all along the face of the bluff in an abrupt mural face, often projecting in advance of the superimposed cliff of magnesian limestone a hundred feet and more: and at the crown of the deposit it forms a perpendicular precipice, without any of those alternate receding ledges which mark layers of inferior durability.

I am not at present in possession of a press suitable

for testing the strength of building stones by the force required to crush them; but, in the present instance, this examination is hardly necessary, since all stonecutters who have worked the Marble Hill rock agree as to its strength and remarkable toughness; surpassing in this respect all other rocks which they have worked from western quarries. They say, too, that it works freely under the chisel, requiring not so much skill and experience in producing ornamental cutting in this material, as in the Italian statuary marble. They agree, too, that it receives a higher polish than any western rock, except the Frankfort birdseye marble, which latter is, however, so brittle, that it is very limited in its application.

In a few of the upper layers of the Marble Hill quarry, at the upper opening, I observed some small specks of sulphuret of iron, a detrimental ingredient, especially in rocks destined for ornamental purposes, both from its extreme hardness and liability to decomposition, leaving frequently a stain around the spot where it was embedded; it also prevents the rock from receiving a uniform polish.

But this mineral occurs only seldom, and then only in small specks here and there in some of the upper layers, and can easily be avoided in selecting the material. Protoxide of iron, which is an ingredient of the rock, to the amount of one and a half to three per cent., is not injurious, since it is united with carbonic acid, and in passing from a lower to a higher state of oxidation, by absorption of oxygen from the air, has rather a tendency to harden the cement of the rock of which it is a constituent. The light yellow spots and lines surrounding the white shells, which contribute to give variety to the colors of the polished surface, are attributable to this constituent, partially oxidized.

I have dwelt somewhat at length on the qualities and properties of this building material, because I consider it a matter of great practical importance, in as much as immense sums of money have been expended for very destructible and inferior materials from quarries in the same county; and the consequence has been that the buildings—some of them public edifices—of which they have been constructed, are fast going to decay, after a few years' exposure, when the same hills might have afforded a building stone that would have withstood the vicissitudes of the atmosphere for centuries.

There are other beds of the blue limestone capable of receiving a polish sufficient to render them suitable for a marble; but, for reasons already set forth, the shell-marble of Jefferson county is to be preferred.

The thickness of the blue limestone formation in Indiana, is between four and five hundred feet. Many of its beds are remarkably rich in fossils, in fact, many layers are but an agglutinated and cemented mass of shells and corals, often in a wonderful state of preservation, affording to the naturalist a boundless field of research into the ancient fauna that peopled this earth during the protozoic or first appearance of life on this planet.*

Having determined the succession of the geological formations along the Ohio river, my next object was to ascertain, by means of the zig-zag lines which I ran for that purpose, the general *limits of the various formations throughout the southern part of the State.*

My observations have not as yet, of course, been sufficintly extensive to point out the direction of these lines in all their meanders; and, indeed, this never can be accomplished. until we shall have accurate topographical maps of the State, on which all the hills and ridges shall be carefully delineated. Their general direction, however, has been ascertained.

Limit of the coal formations.

From Oil creek, the line of junction between the coal formation and underlying sub-carboniferous limestone, runs pretty nearly north, a little west of Paoli, Bedford and Bloomington, thence it bears somewhat more to

---

* The references to sections and fossils, which accompanied the M. S., are here omitted, as they were not published with the text.

the west near Spencer, and crosses the National road near Putnamville.

Since the strata, as has been mentioned, roll with the undulations of the country, patches of the coal formation occasionally make their appearance a little east of this line, but it will never be found extending far beyond it; and, I think, in no instance beyond the second meridian.

Thus the counties of Perry, Dubois, Martin, Greene, Owen, and all the counties lying west of them; besides some of the western portions of the counties of Crawford, Orange, Lawrence, Monroe and Putnam, belong to our bituminous coal formation; hence, in all this district of country, beds of sandstone, clays, shales, seams of coal and occasional patches of limestone are found prevailing.

Limits of the strata forming the sub-carboniferous group.

The various strata which have been described as occurring east of this line, will be found prevailing in a northerly direction, in curved belts running from the Ohio river nearly parallel to the limits of the coal formation. Thus, about Fredonia, Leavenworth, Paoli, Orleans, Bedford, Bloomington, the Falls of Eel and Putnamville, the sub-carboniferous limestone series exist. In Harrison, Floyd, Washington, and part of Jackson, Brown, Bartholomew, Johnson, Monroe, Morgan, and Hendricks counties, the knob-stones are found. In the knobby portions of this district of country the soft siliceous strata of this series are the prevailing rocks.

Extent of the aluminous slate.

The underlying black aluminous slate extends through a great part of Clarke, Scott, Jennings, Jackson, Bartholomew, Shelby, Johnson and Marion counties, towards Indianapolis; but in this neighborhood near the National road, the strata are so completely covered by drift, that it is difficult to detect the original strata. Even the deepest wells have not penetrated through this drift.

Zone of coral limestone.

The underlying coral-bearing limestones of the Falls of the Ohio form a narrow zone extending through part of Clarke, Scott, Jennings, Bartholomew, and probably also under the superficial deposits of part of Johnson and Marion counties.

Magnesian limestone. The magnesian limestones, of upper Silurian date, prevail through the western part of Jefferson, Jennings, eastern part of Bartholomew, western part of Shelby, and probably underlie the superficial deposits of part of Hancock county. The beds extend probably all through the dividing ridge between the waters of the Wabash and Ohio river.*

These magnesian limestones, on account of their resistance to atmospheric vicissitudes, form prominent cliffs where they crop out; hence the name of "cliff limestone" has sometimes been applied to this formation.

FALL SURVEY.

(NORTH OF THE NATIONAL ROAD.)

In proceeding north, on my fall survey, I passed through Greene, Daviess, Martin and Dubois counties, and found them, as I had previously supposed, belonging to the coal formation. I also crossed the limit of the coal formation in four new points: two in Orange county, one in Monroe, one in Owen county.

Extensive diluvium in the north. On crossing the National Road I found the greater part of this northern country covered by a drift of sand, gravel, bowlders and clay, sometimes to a very great depth. For this reason it was only at a very few points where I could obtain a view of the rocks belong-

* A remarkable feature in the physical geography of Indiana is that the summit level of this dividing ridge approaches, north of Madison, within five miles of the Ohio river, where some of the sources of the east fork of White river take their rise.

ing to the carboniferous and sud-carboniferous formations. I discovered, however, that the eastern boundary of the coal formation crosses the Wabash near Attica.

Limit of the coal formation crosses the Wabash near Attica.

North of this point I have not yet been able, on account of the drift deposit, to get a view of the rocks, so as to satisfy myself completely as to the continuation of the line. But from the appearance of the country, the composition of the soil, the nature of the superficial strata, the debris along the lake shore, a chemical analysis of the water, the growth of timber, and other indications, I have reason to believe that it continues on nearly in the same direction beneath the drift. The same is probably true of the other boundary lines. They all appear to run in their general course, in slightly curved lines, more or less parallel to one another, in a northerly direction. These points require, however, further investigation.

This much, however, is probable, that the counties of Parke, Vermillion, Warren and Fountain belong to the bituminous coal formation.

In the bed of Lake Michigan, at the southern extremity, at the northern corner of the State, there exists an extensive bed of stiff, tenacious clay, the result, undoubtedly, of the disintegration and denudation of the argillaceous shales at the base of the sub-carboniferous group, and the underlying black slate, which bordered the southern shores of this lake. It forms so solid a stratum, that even the agitation of the waves hardly affect it, and the water is so clear that fish can be seen in calm weather at great depths.

Clay in the bed of Lake Michigan.

The rolling ridges, which form the southern boundary of the lake, are chiefly composed of a calcareous sand, of much greater fertility than one would at first imagine. It is a remarkable fact, that this sand, taken even 30 or 40 feet below the surface, will produce excellent potatoes, water-melons and pumpkins. I have been told, that when the country was first settled, even at the top of some of the sandy knolls, 60 or 70 feet in height, wild rye six feet high, and a rank growth of wild grass were to be seen.

In all probability the stratum of clay, of which we have spoken, extends beneath the sandy deposits which prevail for some miles back in the country. This would account for the lodging of so much water in numerous small lakes, wet prairies, and extensive swamps, about the Kankakee country.

Remarks on the Mineral Deposits, Soil and Growth peculiar to the different Strata.

(SOUTH OF THE NATIONAL ROAD.)

It has already been stated that the objects of the present survey have been general, rather than particular; but, when there was any probability of discovering a valuable deposit of iron, I instituted a more particular investigation in such localities, believing that a good iron bank is of more intrinsic value to the State, than a mine of gold or silver.

Situation of the Eel river ore.

In two different situations, one near Mr. Williams' mill, on the waters of Doe creek, about two miles from Eel river, in Putnam county; the other on the dividing ridge between the waters of Eel and White rivers, in Owen county, about three or four miles from Eel river, I discovered surface-ore of excellent quality. It is of that variety called by Mineralogists "*the compact hydrated brown oxide;*" and it is known to the manufacturer under the name of "*liver ore.*" It is much of the same nature as that found in Middle Tennessee, between the Cumberland and Tennessee rivers.

The analysis of 100 grains Eel river ore yielded:

Sesqui-oxide of Iron	64.4
Water	16.0
Silica	4.0
Alumina	6.0
Loss	9.6
	100.0

This ore, at least the specimen examined, unlike most of the ores of the hydrated brown oxide, contains no manganese. The above ore, therefore, contains at least 44.5 per cent. of metallic iron, and may be expected to yield 40 per cent. on the large scale in the foundry. This is considered a fair average in Tennessee. The specific gravity of this ore varies from 2.9 to 3.5. Details regarding the extent of this valuable deposit are given in an afterpart of this report.

Another deposit of iron ore, of considerable extent, occurs in the sub-carboniferous formation, a little above the black bituminous aluminous slate, in a ferruginous clay, on a sub-branch of Silver creek, near Providence, Clarke county. Some of this ore is rather of a peculiar mineralogical structure. It may with propriety be called a gravel ore, as it is made up entirely of an aggregation of coarse fragments of hydrated brown oxide. It will not produce as much as the Eel river ore, taking equal bulks of each—although equal weights will probably yield nearly alike; it would be rather more easily reduced, or, in the language of the manufacturer, "work more kindly in the furnace." Its specific gravity is 2.6. Ore near New Providence.

Another variety of ore is found in nodules in a stratum of clay near the same place; it is a carbonate of iron. Its specific gravity is 3.24. No analysis of this ore has yet been made, but its appearance indicates that it will yield from 40 to 50 per cent.

These banks have been purchased by Mr. Barnett, of Louisville, who, I believe, proposes erecting iron-works near them. Bog ore near the National road.

Two other deposits of the hydrated brown oxide have been examined; one on Mr. Lamb's land, on the waters of Fall creek, in Marion county; the other on Mr. Baker's land, on Sugar creek, five miles south of Greenfield. It is a bog-iron ore, occurring in swampy ground. Its specific gravity is 2.7.

The extent o these deposits has not yet been ascertained; more or less ore has been observed, however, to extend over several acres. On Mr. Baker's land the hard ore was dug into at least four feet, and beneath it was found a considerable deposit of sott ore—a mixture of red and yellow ochre.

Numerous masses of the clay iron stone, much of the same nature as that found on Mr. Barnett's purchase, have been discovered elsewhere, in beds of ferruginous clay, occurring both in the carboniferous and sub-carboniferous group.

Ferruginous sandstone on the Iron Hill.

On the Iron Hill, near Crooked creek, 6 or 8 miles from Troy, a ferruginous sandstone occurs in the coal formation. This has been considered good ore by some. That on the surface is too much mixed with sand to be fit for working. Its specific gravity is 2.3. It is possible that by digging good ore may be struck. But I should think the prospects more encouraging if it were in the sub-carboniferous formation, instead of being associated with sandstones.

I have not yet had time to make accurate analyses of these various ores, but intend undertaking them if the survey is continued.

A most valuable deposit of what is called by the Potters *marl*, but what more properly speaking, is a fire clay, for it contains no carbonate of lime, has been opened at Troy, by Mr. Clue, from Staffordshire, England. This material, when first excavated, is quite hard, but by exposure to the air it soon crumbles and falls to pieces. When ground and worked up it is employed for making fire-brick, and saggers, used for the support and protection of the pottery-ware while exposed to the heat of the kiln.

Fire-brick are to be made for sale.

The entrance into the excavation made into this bed is close by the town of Troy; it has been carried into the hill side nearly on a level with high water mark. A thin seam of coal rests upon it.

Mr. Clue, the manager of the pottery, informed me that he has bored in the floor of the passage ten feet into this clay, without finding its bottom; and since the passage itself is ten feet more, the thickness of the bed must be over twenty feet. Mr. Clue considers it the finest deposit of the kind he has ever seen. Imbedded in it are nodules of clay-iron-stone; and it often presents impressions of plants.

Pottery at Troy.

It was the existence of this deposit of clay slate, and the neighborhood of good coal on Deer and Anderson creeks, that chiefly influenced the Company of Potters, lately formed at Louisville, to locate themselves at Troy, in Perry county.

About forty English workmen have been brought out from Staffordshire, and extensive buildings have been erected. The first lot of ware was in the kiln when I visited the place in the month of June. Several good beds of clay have been discovered in the neighborhood by Mr. Clue, fit for the manufacture of stoneware. The finer materials, for porcelain or queensware, are procured from the erroneously called *chalk-banks* on the Mississippi.

Several good seams of coal have been opened in different parts of the coal formation. At present it will suffice to mention a few of them.

Coal near Troy.

Two good seams are worked on Anderson creek, 2 or 3 miles from its mouth; the lower called Rhoades' bank, the upper James' bank. The seams run nearly horizontally into the hill, 50 or 60 feet, above the creek. They are rather thin, not being much over three feet, which renders it inconvenient working the coal, unless the miner be seated on a stool. In Europe, however, seams 22 inches, and even as low as 18 and 12 inches, have been worked by young men and boys.

The specific gravity of this coal is 1.27. It yields by analysis:

Volatile Matter..................................	45 grains.
Coke and Ashes..................................	55 grains.
Coal..........................	100 grains.

On Deer creek, near Troy, there is also good coal, some of it of the variety of *cannel* coal. These coals are used at the pottery, and are considered good.

Coal on White river.

On White river, 2 or 3 miles from Petersburgh, several coal banks have been opened. The seams are upwards of six feet thick, and have a roof shaler. The quality in some is pretty fair, but in other cases it is of too shaly a nature, and contains sulphuret of iron. Its specific gravity is 1.27. An average specimen yielded:

Volatile Matter	46.6
Coke and Ashes	53.4
	100.0

Coal near Terre Haute.

Coal of superior quality is obtained seven miles east of Terre Haute and about one mile south of the National road. The bed is 4 feet thick, or perhaps more, as the bottom of the bed was partly concealed under water when I examined it.

The specific gravity of this coal is 1.24 to 1.3. It yields by analysis nearly the same amount of volatile matter and coke as the preceding.

Coal at Merom.

Coal also crops out of the bluff below Merom, covered by a thick bed of shale.

Coal measure soil.

The soil overlying the strata of the coal measures is variable, as sandstone is the prevalent rock; the siliceous soils occupy, probably, the most extensive area, but the shales and clays, which are the next most abundant in the coal measures, produce by their disintegration coal soils, which though more refractory and difficult to subdue, are nevertheless more durable than the siliceous soils derived from the sandstone. Where the limestone exist, there is always a great improvement in the fertility of the subjacent soil, as the admixture of calcareous matter, derived from their debris, contributes not only an extra supply of lime, but also some phosphoric acid, essential ingredients in all rich soils. The proportion of the latter appears to be greatest when the rock is charged with organic remains, such as fossil shells.

The timber in the regions of the coal measures is for

the most part a mixed growth of oak, hickory, ash, poplar, walnut, sugar-tree, dogwood and red bud, and, where the shales reach the surface, beech.

The soil over the sub-carboniferous limestone is usually more calcareous than those of the coal measures, on account of the prevalence of limestone rocks. On this account it is usually better adapted for the growth of small grain and certain grasses. In the early settlement of this country the region of the middle members of this group was generally supposed to be rather a barren soil, from the stunted growth of the oak and hickory, which marked the belt of country through which this member extended; but experience soon proved that the so-called "barrens" were indeed fertile land—remarkably so where the red underclays existed, that are quite prevalent on such tracts of land.

Besides the blackjack oak, *quercus ferruginea;* red oak, *q. rubra*, and white oak, *q. alba*, there are found in the "barrens" butter-nut, *juglaus cathartica;* black walnut, *juglaus nigra;* dogwood, *cornus florida;* sugar-tree, *acer saccharinum.*

It is stated by the oldest inhabitants, that when the country was first settled, it was for the most part an open prairie district, on which was a luxuriant growth of wild grass, known to them under the name of barren grass, which seemed to have taken possession of the soil to the exclusion of the timber, which subsequently sprung up as the country became settled, while, at the same time, the barren grass died out.

In the region of the sub-carboniferous sandstone, except in the immediate vicinity of the encrinital limestones, the soil is not very productive, less so, perhaps, than any of the soils produced from any of the other formations, at least on the summits and high slopes of the knobs, extending through the country where this rock exists.

In the valleys between the knobs the soil is often stiff Stiff clay soils. and refractory, from the large proportion of clay that enters into its composition, derived both from the grey shales at the base of the knobs and the underlying black slate; but this land is capable of great improvement by a judicious system of drainage and an admixture of calcareous matter from the encrinital limestones, which usually lie convenient in the adjacent hill sides.

Growth in the knobs.

The growths in the knobs are chesnut oak, *quercus prinus palustris;* white oak, *quercus alba;* red oak, *quercus rubra;* black oak, *quercus tinctoria;* a small hickory, *juglaus tomentosa;* black gum, *Nasso sylvatica;* in favorable situations, poplar; on the argillaceous slopes, beech; and in flat and wet positions, elm and sweet gum.

Soils derived from black slate.

In the flat lands based on the black slate the soil is usually cold, wet and spouty, and can be reclaimed only with considerable labor, and a thorough system of drainage.

Beech, *Fagus sylvestris*, is the most abundant growth in these wet lands, but the black slate soils support locally a growth of white oak, overcup oak and black oak.

Soil over coral limestone.

The soil over the coralline Falls-limestone is far superior to that of the preceding two formations, being much more mellow and calcareous.

Growth on coral limestone formation.

The growth on this formation is large red beech, *Fagus ferruginea;* large poplar, hackberry, *celtis crassifolia*, sometimes replaced by black walnut or wild cherry, and black locust, *Robinia pseudo-acacia;* a few buckeye, *Pavia lutea*, with an undergrowth of papaw, *Annona triloba*, and grape vines.

Soil of magnesian limestone

The soil derived exclusively from the magnesian limestones of upper Silurian date is inferior to that resulting from the disintegration of the purer fossiliferous limestones above. These pure magnesio-calcareous soils are disposed to bake, but deep subsoil plowing and efficient drainage are of great service to them.

Growth on magnesian limestone.

The growth over this formation is mostly white oak, of a hard and close texture, highly esteemed by ship builders.

Blue limestone soil.

Beyond a doubt there is no soil superior in fertility to that found overlying the blue limestone and marl formations of the West; especially those derived from its most fossiliferous beds. It is not only a remarkably productive soil, but at the same time durable; for many of the best disintegrate so rapidly to soil, that a new soil is being constantly added, and therefore stores of mineral fertilizers are supplied almost as fast as they can be removed by cultivation. This soil is of an argillo-calcareous character, especially well adapted for blue grass pastures; besides almost any crop that may be suitable to our climate. To the richness of the pasture grounds and the abundant harvests of hay and grain, which these lands produce, is to be attributed the large size and remarkable vigor of the stock raised in the blue limestone counties.

Growth on the blue limestone formation. Beech is the most abundant growth on the blue limestone formation, especially where the marly clays prevail; interspersed with these are found sugar tree, buckeye, linn, white ash, black walnut, poplar and coffee-nut, *Gymnocladus canadeusis*, and occasionally black locust.

Bottom soils. The alluvial bottom lands, being generally formed from the disintegration and washings of a variety of rocks in the adjacent slopes, on either side of the valley, are usually composed of a good mixture of the fertilizing earths, together with a large proportion of organic matter.

Corn lands on Wabash. The bottom lands along the largest river flowing through Indiana, *i. e.* the Wabash, are remarkable for their fertility. There is, perhaps, no region of the West so well adapted, both by soil and climate, for the growth of Indian corn or maize. It is emphatically a corn country; so much so, that it is a well known fact, that so soon as the Wabash boats get out with their corn, the Southern States become so fully supplied, that it immediately affects the whole grain markets of the South.

The prairie bottoms of Sullivan, Vigo and Knox are probably unsurpassed by any corn lands in the West; and the heavy timbered bottoms of Gibson and Posey, when once cleared, are equally productive.

Bottom lands on White river.

The bottom lands of White river, though not quite as extensive as those of the Wabash, are as fertile and more varied in their composition, since White river waters a greater variety of formations.

Most of the water in the northern part of the State seems to be highly charged with carbonate of lime, which it undoubtedly derives from the extensive area which the limestone formations must occupy under the drift. This formation is so universal and deep north of the National road, that they are seldom exposed to view, or reached in sinking wells. Such waters, as soon as the come to the surface, gradually loose their carbonic acid, which acts as the solvent, over the carbonate of lime, and a deposition of the calcareous matter ensues, either as marl or calcareous tufa; this latter is found in some places in large quantities, and becomes for this country a most valuable material; for the limestone rocks, being covered to so great a depth by the drift, are not accessible; the inhabitants, therefore, resort to the calcareous tufa, or the loose limestone boulders, for their supply of lime.

Mode in which calcareous tufa and bog iron ore are formed.

It is in a similar way that the deposits of iron-ore which we find here in marshes, are found.

Extent of the Mishawaka ore.

Some of these ferruginous deposits prove to be very extensive. That at Mishawaka, near the St. Joseph river, is 50 or 60 yards wide, varies from 7 inches to 3 feet in thickness, and has been already traced for 5 miles. It is from this deposit that the Mishawaka furnace is supplied. It is the most compact bog ore I have seen; a great portion of it can only be raised with the assistance of iron wedges and crow-bars.

Bog iron on the Wea and Tippecanoe.

There are similar deposits on the Tippecanoe and Wea, where the ore is of good quality. Their extent has not yet been satisfactorily ascertained; but since they evidently have their origin in the same formation, crossing it in lines running nearly from north-east to south-west, parallel to one another, there is reason to hope that they may be productive.

On Pine creek, in Warren county, I found large

quantities of argillaceous iron ore. It originates in a dark clay slate, similar to that used at Troy for fire-bricks, and no doubt would be suitable for such a purpose; it is associated probably with coal, for seams of coal crop out higher up the creek. From various inquiries which I have made, I expect to find similar ore on Coal creek, in Fountain county; on Sugar creek, in Parke county, and on the Vermillion, in Vermillion county; but these places I have not yet had time or opportunity to explore.

Argillaceous iron ore and clay slate on Pine creek in Warren county.

SUMMARY AND PRACTICAL INFERENCES.

In conclusion to this report the following general summary will be advantageous and useful to the reader:

The leading geological formations of Indiana are:

1. The recent alluvial bottoms, prevalent along our large rivers. *Alluvium.*

2. The drift deposits, overspreading to a great extent the counties north of the National road, and more partially some of the southern counties, particularly in the slopes of the hills adjacent to the large rivers. *Drift.*

3. The coal measures, or carboniferous formation, including a number of valuable beds of bituminous coal, interstratified through 1,000 or 1,500 feet of associate strata of sandstone, shales and occasional limestones. These coal beds vary from 1 to 7 or 8 feet in thickness. *Coal measures*

The area of this coal formation is principally confined to the districts east of the second principal meridian. *Area of coal measures.*

4. The sub-carboniferous limestones, forming a belt of country some 10 to 20 miles in breadth, just east of the coal field. *Of sub-carboniferous limestone.*

5. A fine grained freestone, with subordinate shales, and encrinital limestones, occupying the knobby regions of the State. *Of Knob freestone.*

Of black slate

6. The black slate formation, occupying a narrow zone of flats east of the knobs.

Of coral limestone.

7. Coral limestone, best exposed on the falls, and forming a narrow, fertile, calcareous tract, just east of the above mentioned flats.

Of magnesian limestone.

8. A magnesian limestone, forming a less fertile, cliffy region, east of the preceding.

Of blue limestone.

9. A blue limestone and marly clay formation, the most fertile districts of the State, and occupying the eastern counties, averaging some forty miles from its western boundary to the extreme eastern limit of the State, in the vicinity of the Ohio river, but rapidly expanding towards the north, so that in the upper Wabash country its thickness must be more than double that, or nearly 100 miles.

Drift north of National road

North of the National road these formations are for the most part overspread by deep drift deposits.

No coal east of second P. M.

Even the rapid reconnoissance, at present made, authorizes the assertion, that it would be a useless waste of time, money and labor, to search for coal in any of the counties east of the second principal meridean, or east of the belt of limestones, that succeed to the coal formation on the east; because all experience goes to show that there are no workable beds of coal associated with these limestones, or any of the underlying formations, that crop out to the surface east of that formation. Therefore, *all search for coal in or beneath the black slate formation of Floyd, Clarke, Scott, Jackson, Bartholomew, Johnson and Marion counties may be predicted as fruitless.*

No coal associated with black slate.

Manufacturing districts.

The western counties of Indiana must ultimately become the principal manufacturing districts of the State, from the fact of their geological position within the Indiana coal field; for all experience proves that manufactories have most generally sprung up and flourished in coal regions; this arises from the simple fact that *there* is to be procured the cheapest fuel, the most universal source of mechanical power.

With the proper precautions and experience, excellent freestones for building purposes may be obtained, both in the coal formation, (particularly towards its base,) and also in the knob formation, above the black slate and grey shales. Some of the sandstones at the base of the coal formation are suitable for furnace hearthstones; and near the same geological horizon there are, locally, fine grained silicious rocks, approaching in character to the Arkansas whetstones, and answering similar purposes. There are also beds that will afford good grindstones. Freestones for building.

The shales of the coal measures afford, locally, both argillaceous iron ore and carbonate of iron—ores similar in composition to those from which most of the Scotch iron is produced. Iron stones in local measures.

Towards the boundaries of the coal formation and the subjacent limestones, there are good hematilic iron ores, similar to those worked in Tennessee and Kentucky, in the counties bordering on the Cumberland and Tennessee rivers. Limonite ores.

Since I first called the attention of the proprietors to the deposit of the hydrated brown oxide of iron, near the Falls of Eel river, examinations have been made, by digging in four or five different places. Ore has been struck in all of them; many tuns have been thrown up, and the prospects are so encouraging, that the proprietors of the Falls are now endeavoring to form a company to erect a furnace, and commence smelting the ore on an extensive scale. Ore on Eel river.

These hematilic and limonite iron ores of Indiana occur in the same formation as the rich deposits of the same ores in Tennessee; but those hitherto discovered in Indiana lie higher in this formation than in Tennessee, viz: between the Pentremital and Archimedes beds and the lowest members of the coal measures, whereas in Tennessee they are found chiefly between the barren limestones and the siliceous strata towards the base of this group.

Some of the shales and underclays of the coal measures answer well for fire clays. Near Troy there is a Fire clays.

thick bed of this material, from which fire-brick and saggars can be made.

Potters clay. Some of the clays of the coal formation answer well for the manufacture of stone-ware, grey pottery and queensware.

By making accurate observations on the succession, equivalencies, dip, strike and relative position of the various coal measures in different parts of the State, an observer, experienced in Western geology, will be able **Depth of coal.** to estimate and predict at what depth any given bed of coal, that may be beneath the drainage of the country, can be reached by shafting.

Sub-carboniferous building stone. Many of the beds of the sub-carboniferous limestone make good building stones. Some of the oölitic limestones take a polish and furnish a cream-colored marble.

Copperas and alum. The black bituminous slate at the base of the knobs may be used for the manufacture of alum * and copperas.

Hydraulic limestones. Under the black slate there is a good hydraulic limestone. Hydraulic limestones may probably also be found in the sub-carboniferous group, and amongst the blue limestones.

Magnesian building stones. Some of the buff magnesian limestones under the coral limestones of the Falls of the Ohio are good building stones, but the underlying, banded, "four foot" bed of argillo-magnesian limestone is not to be depended upon.

Shell marble. The shell-marble rock of Jefferson county in the upper part of the blue limestone formation is not only a beautiful marble, but also a durable building material. There are other beds of the blue limestone, that may be used as marbles, as well as for building purposes.

---

* For this purpose it must be heaped together in piles, and set fire to; it will burn for a short time, as we have before explained. After combustion, the sulphur and iron are both oxidized—the former becomes sulphuric acid, the latter, oxide of iron. A portion of the sulphuric acid unites with alumina, and the rest with oxide of iron—forming a double salt—the sulphate of alumina and iron. The iron has now to be got rid of. For this purpose, potash or ley is added, which throws down the oxide of iron, and appropriates its sulphuric acid to itself; thus forming a sulphate of alumina and potash, or alum.

The unmixed soil of the coal measures is less productive than that of the sub-carboniferous limestone. The least productive land is that on the summits and upper slopes of the knobs. The most fertile soils of the State are the argillo-calcareous soils, derived from the most fossiliferous beds of the blue limestone formation in the eastern counties.

Comparative productiveness of soils.

In regard to the soils resulting more particularly from drifted materials, which occupy a great area in the northern part of the State, and on the slopes adjacent to our large streams, it may remarked, that being the transported debris of a great variety of formations we may infer their general fertility, since they must contain a mixture of the earthy ingredients, salts and bases, highly favorable for supplying the required elements for thrifty growth, and must possess, at the same time, the mechanical properties favorable for the retention of moisture, the permeation of air, and for the reception of the nitrogenous principles derived from the atmosphere.

Drift soils productive.

The soil of the country bordering on Lake Michigan, though quite sandy in appearance, is probably rich in calcareous matter, and resting, as it does, on a clay subsoil, is far more productive than its appearance would lead one to suppose.

Soil near Lake Michigan.

The water in the north-western counties is strongly impregnated with carbonic acid. This, acting as a solvent upon limestone, and the protoxide of iron, dissolves them wherever it meets with them in its passage to the surface. And thus we find these waters often highly charged with these two ingredients, forming calcareous and chalybeate springs. As they lose very soon, by exposure to the air, the excess of carbonic acid, which acts as a solvent of these ingredients; and as iron is brought also, by the same exposure to air, to a higher degree of oxidation, and therefore to a more insoluble form, these two causes, acting together, soon produce deposits of calcareous tufa and bog iron ore, so frequently found in that country. The quantity of bog iron ore is, therefore, continually on the increase.

Water in the North highly charged with lime and iron.

Greater part of Indiana once under an ocean.

The greater part of Indiana must have been, at some period of the earth's history, covered by an ocean; for most of the fossils in the limestones are of marine origin.

Prospects for gold in Indiana.

None of the precious metals are likely to be found in Indiana, unless in minute portions in the bowlder drift, or in small quantities in combination with other metals;* because the primitive and metamorphic formations, in which alone productive mines of gold and silver ore occur, do not exist in Indiana. It is true that, in some rare instances, silver is found as a sulphuret and as red silver ore, in such formations as exist in the western country; but I have seen no symptoms of any such in our State. The same may be said of bismuth, tin

---

*The gold of the United States occurs in micaceous and talcous slates, which never contain fossils. Stream gold is, indeed, found in alluvial deposits, but these are never far distant from the parent slates. One or two extraordinary exceptions to the general rule of gold being found only in non-fossiliferous rocks, are instanced by Humboldt. He mentions mines being worked for the precious metals in a limestone corresponding in age to the magnesian limestone of England, and one in a deposit as recent even as the oolitic series.

That brilliant metalic-looking mineral, sometimes of a golden yellow color, and at other times of a silvery white appearance, and often crystalized in cubes, so frequently taken for gold and silver, is iron pyrites, a compound of sulphur and iron. It may be easily distinguished by putting a piece of it pounded on to a shovel, and placing it over the fire. If it be iron pyrites, a suffocating sulphurous smell will be perceived, or, in more common language, it will smell of brimstone, and a dark brittle substance will remain.

The only use to which this sulphuret of iron, found so abundantly in many parts of our state, can be put, is for the manufacture of copperas or sulphate of iron. For this purpose, fragments of the ore are strewed in a convenient situation, so as to be acted on by the atmosphere, when the sulphur becomes sulphuric acid, and the iron, oxide of iron. A small stream of water is made to pass slowly over it, this dissolves the sulphate of iron. This solution is conducted into kettles, and evaporated or boiled down; fragments of iron are thrown in, to unite with and neutralize the free sulphuric acid, which is always in excess; and the salt crystallizes so soon as it has arrived at a sufficient degree of concentration.

The thin, elastic, yellow glistening metalic-looking scales, found in many of the bowlders, are mica, or as it is sometimes improperly called, isinglass.

ore, and native arsenic. The only metals which we need look for, are iron, lead, antimony, manganese, zinc, cobalt, and possibly some varieties of copper and arsenic ores.

It is not likely that anthracite coal will ever be found in Indiana, because that mineral is usually found in proximity to metamorphic rocks or granite. No anthracite coal in Indiana.

Several detached pieces of native copper have been found in the State, one weighing five pounds; but, from the nature of the ore, its occurring in washed gravels, and only in isolated pieces, I have reason to believe that they do not originate in the State. I may add that the kupferschiefer of the German miners, yields, at the mines of Mansfield, in Thuringia, an abundant supply of copper ore. This copper slate is found at the bottom of the new red sandstone formation, which overlies the bituminous coal formation; and copper ores have been found in the carboniferous and mountain limestone. There is, therefore, a possibility of discovering workable copper ore in the formations of Indiana. Detached mass of native copper found.

APPENDIX.

SUGGESTIONS AS TO THE MODE OF CONDUCTING FUTURE SURVEYS.

Suggestions regulating future surveys.

It will perhaps be expected that I should say something respecting what remains to be done in future geological examinations. If it be desired to make a minute geological survey of the State, it would be necessary to make, with the aid of good instruments, correct topographical examinations and maps of all the ridges and water courses, to ascertain the succession, thickness, dip and course of the different strata; to collect diligently fossil organic remains; to analyze carefully all the ores, coal, cements, marl, clays and soils, so as to estimate their intrinsic relative value; to make experiments upon the durability of certain strata for building materials; to polish different specimens of such strata as seem likely to afford good marble; to endeavor to ascertain the correspondence, dip and prevalence of the various seams of coal, and accurately determine their thickness and succession, and those of the intervening strata of sandstone, shale, limestone and clay; to make a general collection of specimens, to be arranged and deposited at the seat of government; to determine the nature and variety of the vegetation peculiar to each formation; and, if means are provided, to make observations on the natural history of Indiana generally; to examine carefully the various species to which the fossils belong, and make a rigorous comparison between them and those found in other parts of America and Europe, with a view of discovering the correspondence between our formations and those of other parts of the United States and the Eastern hemisphere. This is a subject now of the highest interest to scientific men in all parts of the world, as it is to confirm or demolish theories, which materially affect the science of geology, in a practical as well as scientific point of view.

It will at once be seen that this is a work which can be fully accomplished only by the united labors of several individuals, by the expenditure of considerable capital, and by the consumption of much time. Whether Indiana would be warranted in carrying out, at the present juncture, so expensive an undertaking, it is not for me to determine. I can but express my opinion that it would ultimately amply repay all outlays and labor.

A more economical, and, of course, a more superficial and less satisfactory course, might be pursued—a course similar to that which was necessarily adopted during the past season. It would be for the geologist to travel from place to place, make merely occular, or perhaps partial surveys with instruments, of the various beds of rocks, and determine, by approximation, their thickness, dip, succession, &c.; to collect, as far as time and opportunity will permit, specimens and fossils; and to follow up the before mentioned objects, as far as the time and exertions of one individual may suffice for that purpose.

This plan, of course, could not pretend to the same accuracy of detail as the former. Still much that is important might be accomplished. The more extensive plan is that pursued in the Atlantic States, and which, I presume, will ultimately be adopted in Michigan and Ohio.

[END OF PART FIRST.]

CONTINUATION OF REPORT

OF A

GEOLOGICAL RECONNOISSANCE

OF THE

STATE OF INDIANA,

MADE IN THE YEAR 1838,

IN CONFORMITY TO AN ORDER OF THE LEGISLATURE.

BY D. D. OWEN, M. D.,
STATE GEOLOGIST.

PART SECOND.

INDIANAPOLIS:
JOHN C. WALKER, STATE PRINTER.
1859.

GEOLOGICAL RECONNOISSANCE.

To the Honorable,

the Legislature of Indiana:

GENTLEMEN—In fulfillment of my duty as Geologist of the State of Indiana, and in accordance with the instructions contained in an act, entitled "An act to provide for a Geological Survey of Indiana," approved February 6, 1837, I have continued the geological examinations of our State, and beg to communicate to you the results, in the following

REPORT:

Survey still of a general character.

The geological explorations made, during the past year, have still been of a general character, in further prosecution of the geological reconnoissance commenced last year, preparatory to a more detailed survey, if hereafter sufficient means are provided, to secure the necessary assistance and instruments indispensable for a minute survey.

My examinations have, this season, been chiefly directed to those localities, an investigation of which might serve to solve the following important questions in the geology of Indiana:

Geological questions presented for solution.

Do the coal-measures of Indiana contain iron-stones and blackband iron ores such as are obtained and extensively wrought in the Scotch coal fields, which supply the largest proportion of iron consumed in this country?

What course does the Northern extension of the boundary line of our bituminous coal formation pursue?

Does it still partake of a regular curve, indicating that our carboniferous formation is part of a great basin, as hinted in last year's report?

Can our coal be worked extensively without sinking shafts?

Are there any extensive bodies of limestone suitable for public works in our coal formation?

Are any of the sandstones of this formation, except those at its base, fit for building purposes?

Are there, in the coal measures of Indiana, productive beds of iron ore, such as are yielded by many of the equivalent formations in other parts of the globe?

Will other parts of the coal formation in the North yield good fire-clays like those of Perry county?

What are the number and extent of the workable beds of coal in the Indiana coal field, and how far do these lie apart?

Do veins of trap, basalt, or greenstone protrude through any part of our coal strata, causing faults or troubles, so frequent in other coal fields?

Does our bituminous coal formation extend, in any instance, beyond the second principal meridian?

Do workable seams of coal alternate with any of the strata designated in last year's report by the term *sub-carboniferous?*

What formation in Indiana promises to yield the most productive brine?

Are extensive deposits of the hydrated brown oxide of iron, so common in the sub-carboniferous rocks of Tennessee, prevalent in the equivalent formation of Indiana?

Is our sub-carboniferous limestone likely to yield any body of lead ore?

Whence originate the detached masses of native copper which have been found in several parts of Indiana?

In what do the geological formations of Indiana agree

with, and in what do they differ from, the geological formations of the adjoining States?

I propose, first, to record a few detailed observations, under the heads of the individual counties in which they were made: Heads under which observations are recorded.

Secondly, to draw some important comparisons between the geological features of Indiana and those of the adjoining States: and

Thirdly, to sum up the important results of my observations, including practical inferences therefrom.

POSEY COUNTY.

The operations of this year were commenced in the dividing ridge between the Ohio river and Big creek.

Here I have to acknowledge the valuable aid rendered to me by Mr. Philips, the county surveyor of Posey, who voluntarily offered to accompany me in my geological examinations in that county. Having explained to him the objects I had principally in view, his thorough acquaintance with the county enabled him, at once, to take me to the most interesting spots. Thus, in a short time, I succeeded in determining the succession of the strata extending through the centre of the county, and in making also an approximation towards their thickness, as represented in the following section:

Section in part of Posey county.

1. Soil, 2 to 4 feet.
2. Subsoil (and gravel?) 4 to 6 feet.
3. Silicious marl belonging to the Quarternary Period, 50 to 100 feet.
4. Sandstone with carbonaceous streaks and ferruginous at the base, 20 to 30 feet.
5. Shale, a few feet.
6. Fossiliferous limestone, 4 to 6 feet.
7. Black bituminous shale and coal, a few inches.
8. Argillaceous shale with bands of sandstone, both containing fossil plants, 10 to 15 feet.
9. Slaty clay with nodules of argillaceous iron ore, 5 to 10 feet.

10. Shale and bituminous coal*, with iron pyrites, in the bed of Big creek, thickness undetermined; the underlying shales are probably 100 feet or more in thickness.

In the hills adjacent to the Wabash river, in this county, there are shales, sandstone and thin coal, that probably occupy a lower position, geologically, than any of the members of the foregoing section. The succession in the hills on the south-east side of New Harmony Cut-off is as follows:

Section of the Wabash hills in Posey co.

1. Soil and subsoil.
2. Fine, silicious marl.
3. Sandstone used for building.
4. Shale, with cross seams of pencil fracture.
5. Thin coal and shale with concretionary masses of fossiliferous limestone.

No. 2, of this section, contains the following land and fresh-water shells: *Helex fraterna*, *H. hirsuta*, *H. convexa*, *H. indentata*, *H. labyrinthica*, *H. minuta*, *H. perspectiva*, *H. lineata*, *H. monodon*; *Helciana occulta*; *Cyclostoma lapidaria*; *Pupa armigera*, *malania* (rare.)

No. 3, is the sandstone of which the first story of my laboratory is built, quarried in the hills adjacent to the Cut-off dam. The majority of the rock has stood the test of half a century well, except where the walls were exposed internally to the action of salt when the lower story was used as a pork-house, previous to my purchase. Saline efflorescences exert always a very deleterious influence on all building stones; especially on sandstones and freestones.

The fossiliferous concretionary limestone, included in No. 5 of the section, contains: *Pleurotomaria coronula*, *Terebratula pentatomo*, *Productus undiferus*, *Productus Wabashensis*, *Productus Rogersii*, *Bellerophon*, allied to, but probably distinct from, *B. Urii*.

Limestone of Posey county.

The Big creek limestone is of much better quality

*The shale under this coal is probably the horizon of the fossil stumps found on Big creek at Blairsville.

than is generally found throughout our coal formation, particularly the lower part of the bed, which can be procured in large blocks of from 14 to 18 inches in thickness, well suited for building purposes. In some places, the lower blocks of limestone are variegated both with veins and with sections of fossils; and, being sufficiently hard to take a polish, they afford a grey marble of considerable beauty. We detected it in nine different sections; and, being always in the same relative position, beneath the overlying sandstone and shale, there is every reason to believe that it is a continuous stratum.

The coal on Big creek lies too low, so far as we examined it, to be worked without sinking a shaft. Coal on Big creek.

At several places along Big creek, as, for instance, at Black's mill and at Baxter's mill, sections of the slaty clay are exposed, containing many small nodules and thin bands of argillaceous iron ore, and passing above into indurated clay slate and slaty sandstone. From the disintegration of the slaty rock, a stiff tenacious clay has been formed in the alluvium of Big creek bottoms; which, when there is not too great an admixture of calcareous matter, might be manufactured into earthenware. Deposits of clay and argillaceous iron ore.

In the flats of Black river, on section eight, township four, range twelve, there is a deposit of the hydrated brown oxide of iron; as yet, it has only been procured on one place in this section. Hydrated brown oxide in the eastern part of the county.

About four miles from New Harmony, on the farm of B. C. Macey, a bed of marl, belonging to the Quaternary Period, in some places upwards of six feet thick, has been discovered, and is struck at the depth of from three to six feet in almost every situation in this neighborhood. Indeed, it seems to exist universally over the upland, since it is seen also at John Beal's, nearly five miles from Macey's, and in the range of hills half a mile south of the Wabash river, wherever the cuts are sufficiently deep, exposed in the same relative position. The analysis of this marl, given in the appendix, will show its composition. It will prove to be of great value Marl in Posey.

in improving some of the adjacent sandy soils which have been partially exhaused by a frequent repetition of successive crops of Indian corn.

Hydrated brown oxide of iron on Haines' farm.

Near the boundary of Posey and Vanderburg counties, on the farm of Mr. Haines, there exists a deposit of brown oxide of iron, lying above limestone. How extensive this ore may be remains to be determined by future detailed surveys. It has been observed at Diamond Island and on the flats of Black river; at all of which places it is situated nearly in an east and west line.

A small specimen of sulphuret of antimony was found in this county, on a branch of Mackaddo creek at John McGregor's farm; but no body of this ore has yet been discovered.

VANDERBURG COUNTY.

Strata on Big Pigeon.

Along the banks of Big Pigeon creek slaty clays containing nodules of argillaceous iron ore are exposed, overlaid by slaty sandstone.

These beds have much the appearance of No. 7 of the section given under the head of Posey county; but, since the strata rise towards the north-east, it is probable that these are lower beds, and the limestone found in the ridges above is, most likely, for the same reason, an inferior bed of limestone.

The predominating rocks of Vanderburg, under the main limestone of this county, are argillaceous shales and sandstones, occasionally with iron-stones, and containing the remains of fossil plants.

Strata under the limestone of Vanderburg.

Twin coal.

A coal, between two and three feet in thickness, shows itself at a low stage of water on the Ohio river, six miles below Evansville. This is probably a twin coal made up of two members with a clay stratum of 2 to 4 feet between the coals; the total thickness of the different members being 7 to 8 feet. This is, probably, the highest coal, except some of a few inches, in the county, and lies 80 to 100 feet above a workable four-foot coal that might be reached by shafting at almost any point of the river front of Vanderburg county.

Near the centre of T. 5, S. R. 11 W., in this county, from 11 to 15 feet of limestone crops out in a convenient position for opening a quarry for making lime. The limestone rests here on sandstone passing downwards into argillaceous shale, and occupies nearly the same geological horizon as the limestone at West Franklin, in the south-east corner of Posey county. Locality for burning lime.

About four miles south-east of Pigeon, on the road from Evansville to Mount Vernon, there is a considerable bed of flinty chert. I examined this material with a view to ascertain whether it was suitable for the manufacture of porcelain. Some of it is tolerably light-colored; but it is mostly of a grey, or reddish grey tint, and, probably, too much impregnated with metallic oxides, and lime also, to be valuable as a glazing material. However, this cherty flint should be analyzed to ascertain the correctness of these conjectures, derived from external appearance only. Flinty chert.

Some fifteen years since, a boring was commenced on the bank of Pigeon, in the slaty sandstone; it was carried first to the depth of three or four hundred feet, when a brine was procured, from which salt was manufactured for some time. In hopes of reaching a stronger brine, the borings were carried two hundred feet further, when the brine became contaminated with other saline ingredients, which injured its quality, and the well was finally abandoned. I regret that no account has been kept of the strata passed through. The water of the well has been long used by the inhabitants of Evansville and its vicinity as a medical spring. There is no doubt, from its character, that it will prove serviceable as an aperient in many disorders, particularly in mild cases of fever and of gastric and biliary derangement. This water is a saline chalybeate. Salt well. Character of Evansville mineral water.

From the best information, at present, in my possession, the succession and approximate thickness of the strata, under the drainage of the country, in the south- Strata under the drainage.

ern part of Vanderburg county, adjacent to the Ohio river, under the soil and subsoil, is as follows:

1. Indurated argillaceous shale, 10 feet.
2. Schistose argillaceous sandstone, 35 to 43 feet.
3. Shale with segregations of iron ore, 4 feet.
4. Sandstone passing into indurated argillaceous shale, (with fossil plants and, perhaps, locally 1½ feet of coal,) 20 to 40 feet.
5. Dark bituminous limestone.
6. Black shale.

7. Coal, 1 foot 6 inches,	8 feet, twin vein in all.
8. Shale, with imperfect coal, 4 feet 3 inches,	
9. Coal, 2 feet to 2 feet 3 inches,	

10. Fire clay and pyritiferous sandstone, 2 to 5 feet.
11. Limestone, (may be local,) 4 to 8 feet. This is the main Newburg limestone.
12. Shale, with locally 10 inches of coal, in all 4 feet.
13. Schistose, thin-bedded sandstone and tough argillaceous shale, with vegetable impressions, in all 60 to 80 feet.
14. Dark, fossiliferous calcareous band, thin.
15. Coal, 4 feet.

This coal lies from 200 to 220 feet below the drainage of this part of Vanderburg county.

WARRICK COUNTY.

Succession on the Ohio river.

Thin-bedded schistose, argillaceous sandstones are the lowest strata observed in this county on the bank of the Ohio river above Newburg.

Above these is a mottled buff limestone which lies 60 feet above low water of the Ohio river, and 80 feet above a workable coal bed 4 feet in thickness. This is probably the same coal which is visible at a low stage of water on Little Pigeon, brought up there by the easterly rise of the strata, but which dips 27 feet under the bed of the Ohio river at Newburg.

A few feet above the buff limestone is another bed of

coal from 18 inches to 2 feet in thickness, overlaid by fire clay, black shale and dark, carbonaceous, fossiliferous limestone. This coal lies about 70 feet above low water of the Ohio river, and is probably the equivalent of the twin coal mentioned under the head of Vanderburg county, and perhaps the same coal which shows itself below the dam at Miller's mill on Big Pigeon. The upper limestone is surmounted by shale passing upwards into sandstone.

The succession in the southern part of Warrick county is approximately as follows:

Section at Newburg.

1. Sandstone, 25 feet.
2. Shale, 12 feet.
3. Dark bituminous limestone.
4. Black shale.
5. Fire clay.
6. Coal, (Little Newburg coal,) 2 feet.
7. Fire clay and pyritiferous sandstone, 5 feet.
8. Buff limestone 6 to 8 feet.
9. Schistose, thin-bedded sandstone, 30 feet.
10. Slaty clay, with fossil plants, (and locally a thin coal lying about 20 feet above the following,) 46 feet.
11. Main Newburg coal,* 4.4 to 4 feet.

The rate of dip of the strata to the west north-west, must carry this coal from 200 to 220 feet below the bed of the Ohio river at Evansville.

Beneath this coal there is a space of 80 to 100 feet filled chiefly with indurated argillaceous shale, reposing on a bed of coal, some 2½ feet in thickness, which is probably of good quality; 180 to 190 feet below this is another coal, 3 to 5 feet in thickness, of good quality; the intermediate space being filled chiefly with sandstone and shale.

SPENCER COUNTY.

Strata in Spencer co.

The highest ridges in the western part of this county

* This coal lies from 25 to 30 feet under the bed of the Ohio river at the Hutchison bank above Newburg.

are composed of sandstone; while coal, shale and slaty clay are to be discovered in the ravines and hollows. The hills rise to a greater height than in Posey, Vanderburg, or Warrick, although the strata composing them are of inferior origin to any of those in Warrick county.

Coal on Lake Drain.

I saw coal in two places near Lake Drain. It was so much under water, however, that I had not much opportunity of judging correctly either of its thickness or quality. The seams are covered by a very solid shale, containing lumps of sulphuret of iron.

Coals of Spencer county.

The coals of Spencer county are, most probably, the equivalents of the coals above noted, as coming in beneath the main Newburg coal.

The county seat, Rockport, is built on a conspicuous bluff, on the Ohio river, ninety to one hundred feet high, which forms a mural escarpment of sandstone, known by the name of "The Lady Washington."

This Rockport sandstone most likely belongs in the space between the above-mentioned coals.

Between Rockport and Gentersville, two miles south of the latter place, I found some specimens of iron ore; but I have not yet discovered any continuous vein. Several seams of coal crop out in the neighborhood of Gentersville and Jonesboro'. Limestone occurs two miles west of north of Gentersville.

The coal mentioned in my last report, as lying on Anderson, a creek dividing Spencer and Perry, will probably prove to be inferior to the thick bed of sandstone below Rockport. A considerable quantity of argillaceous iron ore occurs along with the deposits of clay associated with this coal.

The exact order of succession of the strata has not yet been ascertained.

DUBOIS COUNTY.

Examination of the so called "Silver Well."

In this county I first directed my attention to a remarkable looking spot, called the "Silver Well," where considerable diggings have been made in search of ore.

On approaching it, I found masses of flint scattered over the surface of the country. The vegetable growth is stunted and thin, similar to that on an old clearing, although the whole was still, I found, in a state of nature.

The excavation first exposed a ferruginous clay, containing small nodules of iron ore. A stratum of flint, however, soon stopped the further progress of the diggings. No silver was found, as might have been anticipated from the geological formation, but some of this flinty rock may prove valuable, as it has the appearance of being tolerably pure silex. Much of it, however, by the application of acid, showed by its efflorescence a small per centage of carbonate of lime. This admixture, if universal, would render it unfit for the use of the potter. Could it be found pure in sufficient quantities, it would be a valuable acquisition to those engaged in the manufacture of the finer kinds of potter's-ware. This article is now the great desideratum wanted at Troy.

The stunted and barren-like appearance of this region originates evidently from the flinty nature of this rock, which, being intermixed with a stiff, tenacious clay, forms the basis of a very thin soil. The wild and barren aspect of the country, occasioned by this peculiarity of soil, together with the appearance, as report will have it, of nocturnal lights, attracted the attention of the "mineral hunter," and induced him to enter on a fruitless search after silver, which, as I remarked in my last report, could hardly be found in the rocks of this part of Indiana.

Formation at Jasper.

In the neighborhood of Jasper, sandstone is the prevailing rock. At the mill on the Patoka, near town, the rock is rather slaty, and contains numerous fossil plants, chiefly *calamites*. A mile or so below the mill, a seam of coal is worked by the blacksmith of the place. It is overlaid by slaty clay, (a kind of fire clay,) exhibiting impressions of fossil plants; the deposit is, however, so much disposed to crumble, that it is almost impossible to collect them. The coal is about two feet thick, and tolerably good. Another seam shows itself half a mile north-east of Jasper. This bed has a roof of sandstone.

Prospects of ore on the Patoka, above Jasper.

The hills continue to increase in height as you ascend the Patoka, and are still capped with sandstone. Specimens of brown oxide of iron are exposed in loose masses on the declivities; I have, however, not yet been able to discover any extensive deposits.

Ores of this description, associated with sandstones, as is the case with the specimens observed in this vicinity, are apt to be too much impregnated with sand; though in thickly settled countries, where labor is cheap and iron ore not abundant, these silicious iron ores may be worked by the addition of sufficient limestone to flux the extra quantity of silica; but such ore is not usually profitable to work and are apt to produce a "cold-short" iron.

Formation at Stewart's mill on the Patoka.

At Stewart's mill, on the Patoka, the sandstones similar to those of the French Lick, and occupying a position near the base of the coal measures, have already acquired the fine grain and white color of the Hindostan whet-stones.

Locality most likely to afford a profitable supply of salt water.

Were the Patoka between Jasper and Stewart's Mill, a more considerable stream, I should pronounce that locality a favorable one for boring in search of salt water. But a better point for such works would, probably, be found on the east fork of White river, about the mouth of Lick creek, where the formation is similar, and a more plentiful supply of water may be expected.

Commencement of the sub-carboniferous formation.

The first appearance of limestone containing Archimedes, indicating the commencement of the sub-carboniferous group, presents itself in the deep hollows about two miles south-west of Stewart's mill.

Grits between the Patoka and French Lick.

The high ridges between Stewart's mill and the French Lick are still composed of the same white sandstone formation which we have just mentioned as belonging at the base of the coal measures. In places, they will afford good grits. In deeply excavated ravines the upper members of the sub-carboniferous group appear.

The boundary, marking the limit of the coal formation, runs through this county, nearly in a north and south course, keeping between half a mile and a mile from the line between Orange and Dubois. Boundary line of the coal formation in Orange county.

Near the termination of the sandstone formation, but rising through the inferior limestones at the French Lick, is a saline spring, strongly charged with sulphuretted hydrogen; so much so, that after sunset in a summer evening, the odor arising from it can be perceived about half a mile from the Lick, and the ground over which it flows is black, owing to the iron which it contains being converted into a sulphuret of this metal. Mineral water at the French Lick.

Those who reside in the immediate neighborhood of this spring, and under the influence of this gas during the months of July and August, are frequently attacked with fever and ague; while those living on the higher ground, and out of the influence of the immediate atmosphere of the sulphuretted hydrogen, remain quite healthy. Unhealthy influence of sulphuretted hydrogen.

This fact, which can be attested by all the inhabitants of this region, seems to prove that the existence of sulphuretted hydrogen in the atmosphere is one of the predisposing causes of intermittent fever.

A qualitative analysis of the water of the French Lick, made at the well, is given in the Appendix. It resembles the Cheltenham Sulphur Spring in the ingredients which it contains. Character of the water of French Lick.

This spring produces a purgative effect on the cattle which are in the habit of drinking regularly at it. It acts, apparently, on the whole extent of the alimentary canal, and has, doubtless, a beneficial effect upon the health of the animal. It is the strongest and most valuable spring I have yet examined in this State.

Adjoining this, and not twenty steps from it, is another spring of a peculiar character. Carbonic acid and lime seem to be the principal ingredients it holds in solution; but, unlike ordinary calcareous waters, it deposits a white sediment along its course, and the water has a strong, disagreeable taste. It is known by the name of "The White Sulphur Spring," and the sediment has usually been considered to be Sulphur.

I think it is more probable, when it comes to be chemically tested, it may prove to be a combination of sulphur and lime, or rather calcium, a proto-sulphuret of calcium being formed. The water does not seem to contain, however, an appreciable quantity of free sulphuretted hydrogen, which is somewhat singular, as the adjoining spring is so highly saturated with this gas.

Mr. Pinnick, who has resided in the neighborhood of these springs for a great many years, assured me that the one depositing the white sediment was perfectly fresh until the earthquakes happened at New Madid, on the Mississippi.

Situation of the Hindostan whet-stones.

Along the brow of a nearly circular ridge, over which the old Hindostan road passes, in the neighborhood of the mineral spring, are the best quarries of whet-stones. The upper beds, namely, those found about fifty or sixty feet from the summit of the ridge, are more slaty and in thinner seams than the lower ones; blocks of almost any size can be procured, from six feet to a few inches thick. It is a remarkably fine grained, white, uniform silicious rock, occasionally variegated with stripes of a light reddish cast.

Appearance of the whet-stone.

In the natural fissures are very hard silicious bands, highly charged with ferruginous matter. These bands often entirely encircle the block in its natural state. Those who have quarried these whet-stones find, as a general rule, that the thicker and harder these ferruginous bands are, the better is the quality, and the evener the surface of the enclosed block. This rock splits remarkably straight; indeed, more like a piece of timber than a stone. The strata lie nearly horizontal in the ridge, and can be reached, apparently, in any situation on the same level. They are not equally good in every situation.

Quality of whet-stones.

Though not equal in quality to the best quality of Arkansas whet-stones, they are nevertheless a valuable material, and have already a good reputation in the market; and it is not at all improbable that a still better quality may be discovered by a minute examination of the geological formation in which they occur.

No regular fossils have been discovered in these strata; but the surface of the natural fissures present, frequently, innumerable small grooves, some tortuous, resembling the tracks of worms; others, very like those of birds. To determine whether these are merely accidental, or actual fossil impressions, must remain for future investigation.

Symptoms of whet-stones.

Beneath these whet-stones the rock becomes gradually more ferruginous, and breaks into small angular fragments. The indications of the existence of this whet-stone rock, or, in the language of the quarrymen, "the blossom of the rock," are square and rhomboidal fragments of sandstone, with even surfaces, which lie strewed on the ground.

A thin seam of coal crops out in this ridge, at an elevation somewhat above the whet-stone strata.

Termination of coal formation.

This series forms the base or termination of our carboniferous formation in this district, and rests upon the series of limestones formerly described under the name of "sub-carboniferous limestones."

HARRISON COUNTY.

Formation indicative of iron ore.

The greater part of this county is occupied by the Barren Limestone subdivision of the sub-carboniferous group; corresponding in geological position to the formation prevalent in the iron regions of Tennessee and Kentucky, lying in the neck between the Cumberland and Tennessee rivers, in the counties of Stewart and Trigg. It crosses the Cumberland river into Montgomery county ; runs thence in a curved course through Kentucky, occupying part of the counties of Todd, Logan, Simpson, Warren, Butler, Edmonson, Grayson, Hart, Hardin, Mead, Bullit, and Jefferson, and then crosses the Ohio river into Harrison and Floyd. This formation may be traced in its whole course by a belt of oak barrens, bounded towards the east by a range of knobs from one to four hundred feet in height.

Throughout these barrens detached masses of siliceous rocks, of the nature of burr-stone, horn-stone, and chert are frequently strewed over the surface, derived partly from segregations which have been weathered out of the adjacent limestones, and partly disjointed blocks, of more or less continuous layers of this material, inter-stratified amongst the limestones. The interstices, between the layers and joints of this siliceous formation, have been filled in with a highly ferruginous argillaceous sediment that has given rise to the deep red clays which frequently form the subsoil in the districts in question; this circumstance contributes greatly to the fertility of the soil of the "Barrens."

Siliceous blocks in the Barrens not drifted.

An idea is prevalent amongst the inhabitants of the Barrens that these siliceous blocks have been ejected from beneath or transported from a distance; this supposition is refuted by the entire absence of symptoms of volcanic action throughout this region, by the angular form of the rocks, and more especially by their being rich in fossils similar to those of the associated limestones; proving conclusively, that they belong to the same formation.

Sink-holes.

The face of the country through these barrens, though generally level, is broken by basin-shaped hollows, commonly called "sink-holes." Underground caves and subterraneous passages are frequent. These evidently are produced by water charged with carbonic acid, which, having the power of dissolving limestone, gradually undermines the superior strata; these, so long as they retain sufficient support, form the roofs of extensive caverns. But when the process is once begun, it proceeds in an ever-increasing ratio, as the surface exposed becomes continually greater; and the atmosphere, by-and by, gaining access, contributes largely to the excavating process;* at last, the superficial strata subside, and form these numerous sink-holes above mentioned.

---

* The Mammoth Cave of Kentucky, in the upper members of the subcarboniferous group, has, no doubt, been formed by such a process of nature.

Though detrimental to the farmer in some respects, by detracting from the area of arable land, these sink-holes often are of great service as reservoirs for stock-water in a region where, from the permeable and cavernous nature of the substrata, the brooks and even smaller rivers disappear from the surface for a long distance, where they form subterranean streams.

Iron ore not so common as in the equivalent formation of Tennessee.

The corresponding formation in Tennessee and Kentucky has yielded large deposits of the hydrated brown oxide of iron. In Harrison county, such iron ore is not so common. I have discovered, as yet, but one considerable deposit of it in this county, and that, not among the barren limestones now under consideration, but on an outlying ridge of the coal formation, on section 30, township 2 south, range 3 east, near Blue river, on the farm of Mr. Hougland.

Outliers of the coal formation beyond the second principal meridian.

It may be proper here to remark, that some outliers of the coal formation extend into this county as far as Blue river, two ranges beyond the second principal meridian—the line assigned, in last year's report, to this formation. They are, however, not out of place; that is, they still lie superior to the sub-carboniferous limestones, and are merely outliers, and therefore do not militate against the general rule, laid down in my last report—*that the body of the coal formation would be found west of the second principal meridian, and superior to the sub-carboniferous limestone.*

Hydraulic limestone.

At the bottom of a bluff on Blue river, near Mr. Wilson's mill, there is a stratum of impure limestone, having a conchoidal fracture, and decomposing in the air, which has all the appearance of a good water-lime. I have not yet obtained specimens, to enable me to examine it experimentally.

FLOYD COUNTY.

The fine-grained sandstone and encrinital limestones of the knobs are the prevalent members of the sub-carboniferous group in this county. The lower members of the barren limestones extend, however, into the western part of the county.

The sections exposed by the cuts on the New Albany and Vincennes Turnpike, as it passes over the knobs of this county, afforded a good opportunity of investigating the suecession of strata, from the black, bituminous, aluminous slate, to the top of the knobs.

Strata in the knobs.

By the assistance of Mr. Owen P. Owens, engineer on this road, who obtained for me some important levels, and by a study of his profiles, I am enabled to give a section, from the bed of Silver creek, where the black bituminous slate is first exposed, to the top of the knobs, with the respective thicknesses of the intervening strata.

Section of the knobs.

1st	Soil' and subsoil.	6 ft.
2d	Soft sandstone, passing into indurated clay state.	15.4
3d	Encrinital limestone containing good building stone.	5.8
4th	Soft sandstone and indurated slaty clay.	259
5th	Ferruginous slaty clay, containing large masses of argillaceous irod ore and carbonate of iron.	193
6th	Iron stone.	2
Total height of knob above black slate.		481

The surface of the black slate on Silver creek is 38 feet above high-water mark on the Ohio river at New Albany.

Rocks beneath the black slate.

From data derived from borings, made by Dr. Clapp, through the black slate, I am enabled to furnish the thickness of several of the underlying strata.

7th	Black bituminous aluminous slate.*	104 ft.
8th	Crystalline limestone, uppermost layer at the Falls.	8.8
9th	Water-lime.	14 ft.
10th	Hard semi-crystalline coral limestone, (celebrated for its fossils.)	40 ft.

* In other situations the black slate is only fifty feet thick.

There evidently exists a considerable quantity of iron ore in the ferruginous slaty clay lying above the black slate, and since this stratum seems to prevail almost universally in the base of the knobs, the presumption is, that it will yield considerable beds of ore. Those formerly mentioned, as occurring on the Muddy Fork of Silver creek, originate in this stratum.

The above inference seems the more probable, since the corresponding member of the lower sub-carboniferous group in Bullitt county, Kentucky, yields ore in abundance, sufficient to supply furnaces. I should therefore recommend this formation of Floyd county to the attention of the iron-master.

CLARK COUNTY.

The black slate of Floyd extends for about threc miles into this county. On the Muddy Fork of Silver creek, on Section 112, the fossiliferous strata of the Falls of Ohio come to the surface, and continue until Fourteen-Mile creek. At Charlestown it is well exposed, and affords a fine opportunity of collecting a variety of interesting fossils; drawings and descriptions of which can be furnished, if required, for publication.

Saline spring at Charlestown.

In the neighborhood of the Bald knob, about one mile from Charlestown, a saline spring rises through the limestone. The appropriate tests show, in this water,

Chloride of sodium, (common salt,)
Muriate of magnesia,
Bi-carbonate of lime,
Bi-carbonate of magnesia.

Overhanging cliffs formed of the magnesian and coral limestones.

At Work's mill on Fourteen-Mile creek, a section is exposed of the strata lying beneath the last-described fossiliferous beds. These are the equivalent of the "Cliff-limestone" of Dr. Locke: called so by him because projecting and overhanging cliffs are apt to be formed wherever these rocks exist. Most of the rapids and falls in the State are produced by the out-crop of these and the overlying, siliceous, coral limestones.

Fossils are not abundant in these strata. The most characteristic is, probably, a trilobite which occurs in the compact, magnesian limestones of the group allied to, if not the same species, as the *Calymene Blumenbachii* found in the Dudley limestone of Great Britain. There are also some large *Orthoceratites* in the more earthy beds beneath.

JEFFERSON, SCOTT, JENNINGS, RIPLEY, DECATUR, RUSH AND SHELBY COUNTIES.

The formation in these counties being nearly the same, may with propriety be treated of under one head.

Magnesian limestones in the elevated ridges.

The upper part of the elevated ridges in Jefferson, Ripley, Decatur and Rush are occupied by the magnesian and burr-stone beds of Upper Silurian Date; as well as in the eastern part of Scott, Jennings and Shelby; but the black slate extends some distance into the western portion of these latter counties.

Best building stones of the group.

The best quarries for public works may be opened in the pure magnesian limestones of this formation.

Selection of building materials.

Beneath these, where the creeks have cut sufficiently deep, the blue, fossiliferous shell-limestones, alternating with clays, marls and marlites, are exposed.

Sections of hills near Madison.

A section in the cut of the Railroad behind Madison, as given beneath, will give, approximately, the thickness and relative position of these rocks.

1. Buff and grey magnesian limestones of Upper Silurian Date, nearly 100 feet.
2. Marls and clays, 3 feet.
3. Impure, variegated magnesian limestones, sometimes with green and reddish bands, 35 feet.
4. Dark marlite, containing Favistetta and crystallizations of pearlspar, 27 feet.
5. Fossiliferous limestones, alternating with marl, marlites and clays, of Lower Silurian Date, to low-water mark, about 340 feet.

Some of the beds of both No. 3 and 4, of the above section, possess hydraulic properties.

The lower members of No. 5 extend still beneath the bed of the Ohio river.

The strata which have been usually selected for building stones are included in the third group of the above section. But, as I endeavored to impress on the readers of the first part of this report, they are by no means to be relied upon as durable materials, and are far inferior in durability to the compact, buff and grey magnesian limestones, that overlie them, containing the previously mentioned fossil *calymene* (*Blumenbachii?*) In fact some of the impure "banded-beds" have hydraulic properties and might be used for that purpose, but such rocks, in their unburnt state, scale, crack and decompose when exposed to frost and atmospheric vicissitudes so easily that in a few years they become completely effaced, and the structures composed of them gradually crumble, decay and become undermined.

Banded-rock, hydraulic.

The burr-stone mentioned in the first part of this report, which is wrought for millstones in Jennings county, is a member of the upper division of the preceding section.

SWITZERLAND, DEARBORN, FRANKLIN, UNION AND FAYETTE COUNTIES.

Termination of cliff strata in Indiana.

Formation in the eastern counties south of the National Road.

In this part of Indiana, the dividing ridge between the waters of the Wabash and those of Ohio, may be considered the eastern boundary of the magnesian limestone group of Upper Silurian Date. On the western borders of Franklin and Fayette counties these rocks are occasionally to be seen; but the greater part of these two counties, as well as the whole of Switzerland, Dearborn and Union, is occupied by the inferior blue, fossiliferous, shell-limestones and alternating marls. These rise to their highest elevation near the eastern limit of Indiana, and decline towards the east as they pass into Ohio.

I had the pleasure of exploring the region lying along the common boundary-line of the two States, from the Ohio river to Union county, in company with Dr. Locke, the Geologist appointed to explore the western counties of Ohio. Our chief object, during this excursion, was to trace the extent of the magnesian limestones, and to determine whether there was any continuous chain of connection between the rocks of Upper Silurian Date in Ohio, and the corresponding strata of Indiana.

No continuous chain of connection between the cliff rocks of Indiana and those of Ohio in these counties.

The result of our observations proved the correctness of the limit I formerly assigned to that formation in this portion of Indiana.

Vein of ore in Dearborn.

In the forks of Tanner's creek, in Dearborn county, I discovered a vein of the hydrated oxide of iron, running north-east and south-west. It crosses the road on the farm of Mr. Siddle. It is not sufficiently exposed to enable me to form a correct opinion of its thickness and extent.

Small specimens of sulphuret of lead found in Dearborn county.

Small portions of sulphuret of lead have been found on the farm of Mr. Dowden, on the west fork of Tanner's creek, in Dearborn county; but there is no appearance of there being a body of it; indeed, I have reason to believe that the small specimens found originated in a bowlder.

Drift becomes extensive near the National Road.

As you approach the National Road, the drift becomes extensive. On the high ground, erratic blocks, gravel and other drifted materials are the only rocks to be seen; the limestone formation is only visible now and then in the banks of the creeks.

Organic remains in blue limestone formation.

These counties are remarkably interesting to the Geologist on account of the numerous marine fossils found imbedded in the blue limestone formation; some of them are in a wonderful state of preservation, and so abundant that the rock is, in fact, almost an agglutinated mass of marine shells and corals, which lived, died and became entombed in the sediments and precipitates forming in the ocean during the earliest period to which geologists are able to trace back organic existences.

WAYNE COUNTY.

Section on White Water,

The formation of this county is chiefly drift. The

cuts of the National Road, in the bank of White Water, have, however, exposed sections of underlying limestone formations. The principal stratum disclosed appears to be the one given in the last section as the 4th in the series, namely, the dark marlite. Here it is richer in fossils than elsewhere. This marlite is entirely unfit for the builder, but may, perhaps, possess hydraulic properties. Beneath it is a blue limestone, which is tolerably well suited for building. The rock used in the masonry of the bridge at Richmond has been procured from this stratum. I perceive, however, that it is difficult to give a good permanent face to the rock, on account of the numerous projecting fossils imbedded in it. near Richmond.

At the Falls of Short creek, at Moore's mill, and at the Falls of Elkhorn, in this county, I detected some of the members of the magnesian limestone group of Upper Silurian date for the first time since leaving the dividing ridge between the waters of the Wabash and Ohio. This seems to be a continuation of the equivalent formation which occurs at Eaton, in Ohio, about ten or twelve miles from here. This point is, probably, its western termination in this district of country; if so, there must be a distance of eighteen or twenty miles from Elkhorn to Fall creek, in Fayette county, where this group is absent. Strata on Elkhorn and Short creek.

Near Richmond, iron ore of tolerably fair quality has been discovered, but, as yet, not in sufficient quantities to be of any practical utility. Iron ore near Richmond.

COUNTIES NORTH OF THE NATIONAL ROAD, AND EAST OF THE SECOND PRINCIPAL MERIDIAN.

An extensive drift extends throughout these counties; and the sub-carboniferous formation, which underlies it, is but seldom exposed, and then only in the beds and banks of the most considerable streams. My examinations were directed chiefly to these points.

The first appearance of a ledge of rock, on the west Commencement of rock on west fork of White river. Rock below Muncietown. Rock at Andersontown.

fork of White river, is at McIntyre's in Randolph county. It lies low, and is difficult of access. A little below Muncietown, in Delaware county, it is better exposed, and building rock can be procured, though only in thin layers. At Andersontown it becomes a little more elevated above the water, and a tolerable building rock is procured, both on the river and in a prairie some three miles south, on the road to Pendleton.

Rock at Pendleton.

The best section that I have yet seen is in Madison county, at the Falls of Fall creek. The uppermost layer which is struck in digging wells at Pendleton is a variegated limestone, which, if it could be conveniently quarried, would, I think, afford a variegated marble. Below this the rocks are of a siliceous character. One bed, which appears below the Falls, is probably the equivalent of the Sand creek burr in Jennings county. It seems to me rather softer here than on Sand creek.

Gritstone equivalent to Schoharie grit.

The white grit-stones, under the calcareous rocks at the Falls of Fall creek in Madison county, containing caudal shields of trilobites and *conocardium*, most likely belong to the same geological date as the Schoharie grit of the State of New York, which, with the exception of the cauda-galli-grit, is probably one of the lowest rocks of this country referrable to the Devonian system of European geologists.

Some of the whitest of this gritstone might, perhaps, be fit for making glass, if the chemical analysis which should be made of this rock only shows traces of iron and lime. Some of it might also be useful as grindstones for some purposes.

Rock on White river in Hamilton county.

In Hamilton county, on White river, between Noblesville and Strawtown, a ledge of rock is visible; but it lies too low, is too slaty in its structure, and too irregular on the surface, to be valuable.

Rock on Pipe creek, in Madison county.

Also, at several localities on Pipe creek, in Madison county, I discovered strata of rock; none of it, however, is very suitable for building. Near Mr. Atcheson's mill it has the external appearance of a water-lime.

The Wabash, Little river, the Mississinewa, and the

Salamanie, are the only other rivers that afforded me an opportunity of investigating the rock formation under the drift.

The first appearance of a limestone formation on the head waters of the Wabash, is about ten or twelve miles west of the Ohio line;* it is a siliceous limestone, effervescing moderately with acids, and when burnt, it is apt to run into a milky slag. The Wabash then flows almost uniformly over ledges of rocks, for about one hundred miles, to Delphi, in Carroll county. First rock on the head water of the Wabash.

In the bed of Little river, one of the head waters of the Wabash, rock is first seen in Huntington county, on section 8, township 28 north, range 10 east. A little below this I found it exposed above low water. It has very much the character of the Sand creek and Fall creek burr-stone already alluded to. Rock on Little river.

South-east of this, on section 34, township 28 north, range 10 east, similar rock is seen; it is here rather more compact and less porous than on Little river. Over it is a siliceous and variegated limestone, with veins of crystallized carbonate of lime, similar to the bed of rock struck in digging the wells at Pendleton. Some of it, I find, has specks of oxide of iron disseminated in it, and sometimes flinty nodules; if this be universal, it would detract from its value as a marble; but if it can be procured free from these impurities, it would look well when polished.

Most of the exposures of rock on the upper Wabash country above mentioned belong doubtless to the age of the Devonian and Upper Silurian Period; but on account of the difficulty of gaining access to them it will require more minute surveys than have yet been made to ascertain the lines of demarkation between the different groups.

Between Huntington and La Gors, the strata are well exposed by the excavation of the Wabash and Erie Canal. Most of the rock is an argillaceous limestone; and, Water-lime between Huntington and La Gros.

---

* A well dug at Fort Recovery is 30 feet deep, yet no rock was struck.

judging from the fracture and external appearance, will, no doubt, yield in many places a good water-cement.

At the mouth of the Salamanie, and near Logansport and La Gros, the best building rock.

The strata which will supply the best material for building locks and other public works, are those at the mouth of the Salamanie, near Logansport, and between that place and Georgetown.

The quarries two or three miles below Logansport, on the north side of the Wabash, furnish rock which is very similar to that procured on the Muskakituck in Jennings county, and is probably its equivalent.

Rock near Lockport.

The strata near Lockport afford a durable rock in large, though not very thick slabs. They present rather a rugged surface, on account of the numerous siliceous fossils imbedded in them. The organic remains are generally the same as those found on the Falls of the Ohio; and, without doubt, the two formations are equivalent.

Rock near Delphi.

Below this, in the neighborhood of Delphi, the rock becomes very siliceous, and can only be excavated in unshapely masses. Here the limestone formation terminates.

Cliff strata the prevalent rock in the north-east, below the diluvium.

The whole of the rock formation which I have just been describing, I consider as belonging to the strata inferior to the black, bituminous, alumnious slate, and belonging to the Devonian and Upper Silurian Periods of European geologists.

Localities of ore in the north-east counties.

The only important mineral deposit observed as yet in these counties, is bog-iron ore. The localities where I witnessed the most striking symptoms of such ore, were on Calvin creek, in Randolph, near Noblesville, in Hamilton, near Peru, in Wabash, and near Fort Wayne, in Allen. Mr. Mendenhall thinks that the prospects on

Ore on Calvin creek.

Calvin creek are so encouraging, that he has had serious thoughts of commencing the iron business. Unfortunately, when I visited that section of country, he was from home. I examined, however, the swampy ground along the banks of the creek, and observed at one place good ore within about a foot of the surface. In several places, where large trees had been blown down, I discover ore attached to their roots. Judging from these appearances, and from the number of springs which deposit large quantities of hydrated oxide of iron, I am led to believe that the deposit is extensive. But, since all these indications are, of themselves, rather uncertain, I should, by all means, advise a thorough examination by probing, digging, and laying open the ore to its whole depth in several distant points, before any expense is incurred in preparations for the erection of works. Nothing is so mortifying, though not of unusual occurrence, as to find but a limited supply of ore, after expending time, labor and capital, in the erection of an expensive iron establishment.

Ore near Noblesville.

The iron ore in Hamilton county lies on the farms of Judge Finch and Benjamin Purdum, four miles from Noblesville. It has been traced for half a mile, extending in breadth from fifteen to thirty rods, and varying from eighteen inches to two feet from the surface. Its thic'ness is not known; the quality is pretty fair.

Extent of ore near Fort Wayne and Peru.

I endeavored, with a probing auger, which I had made for the purpose, to form some opinion as to the extent of the deposits of ore in the neighborhood of Fort Wayne and Peru. These investigations incline me to believe that iron ore does not exist, in an accessible position, to any great extent, though there may be an extensive bed deeply seated in the earth.

CARROLL COUNTY.

In this county, below Delphi, the black, bituminous, aluminous slate, the equivalent of that described as occurring on Silver creek, in Floyd county, shows itself for the first time in descending the Wabash, where it overlaps the rugged siliceous limestone of Devonian date, the equivalent of the coral limestone of the Falls of the Ohio.

Black slate on Deer creek.

On Deer creek and at the Falling Springs, this argillaceons deposit is exposed to the depth of from thirty to forty feet. One cut at the Falling Springs is thirty-seven feet and a half through the black slate, which is still discoverable beneath, in the bed of the Wabash.

Extensive beds of calcareous tufa at the Falling Springs.

Large deposits of calcareous tufa have been formed here on the bank of the Wabash. Water, highly charged with bi-carbonate of lime, running off from the upper surface of this black slate, has gradually deposited the carbonate of lime in huge, porous masses, and incrusted therewith the perpendicular face of the layers. This recent formation presents beautiful impressions of leaves, roots, grasses, and plants of various descriptions.

Vein of oxide of iron on Paint creek.

Oxide of iron shows itself on Paint creek, in Carroll county, in several places. A continuous vein of this ore seems to run for nearly two miles. This region deserves the attention of the iron manufacturer.

Black slate the formation in Carroll co.

The whole, or nearly the whole, of the western portion of Carroll county is underlaid by the black slate above mentioned. It is, however, for the most part, hidden from view by drift deposits. It extends also into Tippecanoe county, and is seen at Americus, where the cut of the canal has exposed it.

MONTGOMERY COUNTY.

Formation on Sugar creek.

The greater part of this county is underlaid, beneath the drift, by soft siliceous sandstones; the equivalent of the freestone of the knobby region of Floyd and Washington counties. Sections of this formation are exposed along the banks of Sugar creek. Four miles below Crawfordsville, at the mouth of Aufield's creek, a stratum, some four to eight feet thick, of encrinital limestone is exposed. This is the equivalent of the bed of limestone marked 3d, in the series of the section which represents the strata in the knobs of Floyd county.

Encrinital limestone.

These limestones are remarkably rich in remains of *crinoideæ*, and would no doubt be valuable both for the manufacture of lime and as a mineral manure applied to land, either in the ground or burnt state.

Limestone on Sugar creek below Crawfordsville.

Limestone has hitherto been scarce in this neighborborhood, and recourse has been had to calcareous tufa for a supply of lime. The above mentioned stratum will, no doubt, remedy this deficiency, by affording an excellent lime, and likewise, I believe, a good building rock, which is also very much wanted in this county; as the soft freestones above and below this bed of limestone are, generally, not durable.

The boundary line of the coal formation crosses within a very short distance of the south-west corner of this county.

FOUNTAIN, PARKE AND VERMILLION COUNTIES.

These three counties belong to the coal formation, except some nine or ten sections in the north-east corner of Parke, and about forty sections in the east and north-east part of Fountain. The drift is still extensive here, although not so much so as in the counties north and east of them. The best sections of the strata are on the Wabash river, and on Coal, Sugar, and Raccoon creeks, and open to view a rich mine of mineral wealth.

These counties belong to the coal formation.

The first and most easterly outcroppings of coal on Coal creek are near the Forks, about the middle of Fountain county. It is nearly two feet thick, and is overlaid by sandstone, with dark carbonaceous spots in it. There is a little shale below, which passes into slaty clay.

Coal on Coal creek in Fountain co.

About a mile and a half above this, there is also a seam of coal of the same thickness as the one above described, probably a continuation of it. Here, however, it is of better quality than at the former locality, and is fit for blacksmiths' use.

On Miller's Run, a mile from Covington, a seam a little over a foot thick is visible.

Near the mouth of Coal creek, on the Wabash, in Fountain county, no less than six beds of coal are exposed, one above the other, alternating with beds of slaty clay and fire-clay, in which quantities of argillaceous iron ore and carbonate of iron are imbedded. I subjoin a section, showing their relative positions and thickness.

Section on the Wabash just above the mouth of Coal creek.

		ft. in.
1st	Sandstone,	8
2d	Good coal, No. 1,	1.6
3d	Slaty clay and shale,	10
4th	Good coal, No. 2,	1.6
5th	Slaty clay,	10
6th	Shale, or variegated marl,	3
7th	Good coal, No. 3,	1.6
8th	Slaty clay and shale,	8
9th	Slaty clay, interspersed with argillaceous iron ore—bands of ore 3 to 4 inches thick,	5
10th	Good coal, No. 4,	2
		ft. in.
11th	Fire-clay—white above, dark below,	8
12th	Hard bituminous limestone,	6
13th	Main coal, No. 5,	4.6
14th	Soft sandstone, with specks of carbonaceous matter—passes into indurated clay slate,	15
15th	Coal, No. 6. Beneath the bed of the Wabash; thickness not known.*	

* This coal is reported, from borings made for salt by Mr. Thomas, as 12 feet in thickness, and to lie at a depth of about 60 feet below No. 14 of the above section. This thickness probably includes the overlying shale, since we know of no coal measuring that thickness in our Indiana coal field; and this coal is, doubtless, the same as one of the lower coals which reaches the surface in Fountain county.

This section presents a variety of valuable deposits. Several of the argillaceous beds, besides the 11th, will, I think, yield good fire-clay; but a further and more detailed examination will be necessary, in order to determine its real value.

Beds of nodular iron ore may also be found in some of the other intercalated shaly beds concealed by slides and debris on the face of the slope. The iron ore is abundant and of good quality; but these ores should be carefully analyzed to ascertain the per centage of iron and other substances they may contain. The bed of coal, No. 5, is not quite so good as the superior thinner seams.

This section is particularly interesting, since successful borings for salt have been commenced just beneath these strata, a short distance up Coal creek, which will be further noticed in an after part of this report.

Grits on Sugar creek.

On Sugar creek, in Parke county, the coal formation commences at Rice's mill. The country, though generally level on the high ground, becomes abrupt, hilly, and cut into deep ravines on approaching Sugar creek, and presents fine sections of the stratification. The first ridge of the coal sandstone at Rice's mill affords good grits; and on the spring branch, which has laid bare on the adjoining ridge, a thick argillaceous stratum, large quantities of carbonate of iron are seen in the bed of the stream and on the declivities of the ravine.

Carbonate of iron on Sugar creek.

Good coal on Roaring creek.

Three miles below the Narrows, Roaring creek, a branch of Sugar creek, has cut through several seams of good coal. Two of these beds lie close together, and are separated only by about two feet of shale. The upper one is about three feet thick; the lower, four feet or more. These are probably the most important workable seams on this branch; but above and below them, are several others, not, however, sufficiently exposed to show their exact thickness.

Here would be a good opportunity of manufacturing copperas and alum, especially when the coal comes to be extensively mined. Nature herself has formed under an overhanging cliff of sandstone—beneath which is an aluminous and pyritiferous slate—bushels of copperas and sulphate of alumina, sometimes in the form of delicate and beautiful crystals.

Carbonate of iron on Roaring creek.

The argillaceous deposits on Roaring creek will afford, also, large quantities of carbonate of iron—some of the bands of this ore are three to four inches thick, and numerous. A great proportion of the loose rocks in the bed of the stream, some distance above its mouth, are carbonate of iron.

Black limestone on Square Rock creek.

On Square Rock branch there occurs a stratum of black limestone, varying from six to twelve inches in thickness. Beneath it is slaty sandstone, shale, and a seam of coal some five to six inches, resting on variegated shale. The limestone deserves notice on account of its durability. Most of the dark limestones of our coal formation are much disposed to crack and scale off. But the edges and angles of the detached blocks of this rock, long exposed to the action of air, water and sun, are angular and sharp, and very few of the rocks are at all cracked. This limestone could be quarried very conveniently in some places.

Variegated shales.

Reddish or variegated shales, characteristic of the salt regions of the western country, are not uncommon on this creek.

In passing along the banks of Sugar creek to the foundry, I observed several minor seams of tolerable coal, too thin to work.

Coal of the Sugar creek foundry.

At the Sugar creek foundry, six miles below the Narrows, in Parke county, there is a seam of coal three feet thick, resting on slaty clay, and having a roof of solid sandstone. This coal is mined for the use of the foundry, and yields the best coal and coke I have yet seen in the state; as good, indeed, as I have seen in the western country. Its structure in the bank is columnar, and the fracture conchoidal, like that of cannel coal; its lustre glistening, resinous; it receives a polish; it takes fire, and burns with a clear yellow flame, melting slightly and caking together. It is so clean, that it would not soil a cambric handkerchief. The seam lies high, and having a solid sandstone roof, it can be worked very conveniently. An analysis of this coal is given in the appendix.

A fine fire-clay is procured close to the foundry. The trials which have been made of it prove it to be equal, if not superior to any yet known in the western country. The cupola, which is lined solely with this clay, has been in blast for three years, and has only been renewed once.

Dark limestone at Perrysville.

At Perrysville, in Vermillion county, a bed of dark limestone, from four to six feet thick, is the most prominent feature in the stratification on the banks of the Wabash. It has all the appearance of being the same bed as that observed in the section on the Wabash above the mouth of Coal creek, in Fountain county, marked the twelfth in the series, superincumbent on the four foot and a half seam of coal.

At Perrysville I observed shale beneath this dark limstone, but no coal could be discovered. Over the limestone is a ferruginous clay, containing some nodules of argillaceous iron ore. It is to be regretted that this stratum of limestone is much disposed to crack in the sun, as it could be got out in fine large blocks.

The coal in this part of Vermillion county is principally procured from Mr. Hughes' bank, on the coal branch of Vermillion river. The following is a section of the strippings at this bank:

Section at Hughes' bank

		Feet	in.
1st	Shale.	1	6
2d	Good coal.	2	
3d	Fire-clay.	1	6
4th	Coal.	0	3
5th	Fire-clay.	1	8
6th	Coal.	4	6

The lowest seam of coal is of similar quality to the four foot and a half seam at the mouth of Coal creek.

On Vermillion river, four miles above Eugene, a similar series of coal and fire-clays is exposed, surmounted by a thick bed of sandstone.

Below the mill at Eugene, a thick stratum of dark limestone is visible—probably a continuation of the same noticed at Perrysville and the mouth of Coal creek.

In Vermillion county, about six miles south-west of Clinton, on section 23, township 14 N., range 10 W., near Brouillet's creek, there is the finest prospect of iron ore that I have yet seen in Indiana. The iron ore is of two kinds: the argillaceous iron ore, (called shell ore by the iron masters,) and carbonate of iron. The first is found in a more or less continuous bed from three to four feet thick, resting on a highly ferruginous limestone, and covered only by a thin stratum of soil.

Ore on Brouillet's creek.

Judging from the number of places where I saw the ore cropping out on the banks of Brouillet's creek; from its being always in the same relative position with respect to the underlying ferruginous limestone; from the growth of timber, peculiar throughout this iron region; and from the quantity of gravelly ore in the bed of Brouillet's creek, it must be extensive. At least two thousand acres of ground are underlaid by this ore; indeed, the same vein has been seen at two points six miles apart.

The carbonate of iron originates in argillaceous deposits, which lie higher up Brouillet's creek. This ore also must be in large quantities, from the indications observed along the banks and beds of the stream.

The argillaceous iron ore is of a quality that will work very easily in the furnace, and produce a metal of superior quality, similar to the Juniata iron. It is well known to iron masters that a mixture of two kinds of ore is preferable to working one kind by itself. The mixture that can be produced here will be highly advantageous: both will work better, and produce more than either ore would singly.

The ferruginous limestone beneath the vein ore may be used to great advantage as a flux, because it will not only afford the lime necessary to flux the clay in the argillaceous iron ore, but will also furnish a percentage of iron, in aid of the products of the furnace. **Ferruginous limestone beneath the vein of ore.**

An analysis of the ore and limestone will be made and given in the Appendix, showing the percentage of iron in each.

On section 22, township 14 N., range 10 W., and close to ore, (for it is found also abundantly in this section,) is a bed of fine coal, which is exposed at one place 8 feet; how much deeper it extends is not known. The same seam has been seen in sections 26, 27, 28 and 35. **Good coal upwards of eight feet thick on section 22.**

On section 22 I observed also an under-clay, which promises to afford good fire-clay. **Fire-clay on section 22.**

Although I have not seen sandstones in this county which I considered suitable for furnace hearth-stones, I have no doubt, from the position which Vermillion occupies in the coal formation, that such can be found—if not in the county, at any rate in the adjoining counties of Parke and Fountain—for most of the hearth-stones used in West Tennessee are procured at Golconda, which occupies a geological position analagous to the one in these counties.

When we consider the geological formation of this locality; the quality, variety and extent of the ore; the cheapness with which it can be stripped and carried to the furnace; the thickness, extent and quality of the coal; the character of the limestone to be used as a flux; the prospects of fire-clay; the heavy growth of hickory and oak on the upland, besides the variety of other fine timber in the bottoms; the general levelness of the country; the short distance from thence to the largest navigable stream in the State; the richness of the arable soil; the absence of competition in the iron trade in Indiana—there is here, certainly, a combination of circumstances very favorable for the reduction of ore and the carrying on of all the branches connected with the manufacture of iron.

CLAY COUNTY.

This county occupies the same geological position as Parke and Vermillion,—bordering on the eastern confines of our coal formation, and promises to afford a similar variety of mineral productions. The drift is less extensive here, and therefore the carboniferous formation is more frequently exposed.

Coal or ore in Clay county. On a branch of Eel river, about a mile from Bowling Green, there is a bed of good coal, from four to five feet thick. In the neighborhood of it there is also a vein of iron ore, partially exposed.

These are the only important mineral deposits which I have yet observed in Clay county. My examinations here, have, however, not yet been much in detail.

GREENE, MARTIN AND PERRY COUNTIES.

These three counties, like the preceding, also skirt the borders of the coal district, and belong entirely to this formation. As the remarks which I have to make upon the geology of these counties are of a general character, and apply in common to all the counties lying at the base of our coal formation, I defer them until I make my general remarks.

VIGO, SULLIVAN, KNOX, DAVIESS, PIKE AND GIBSON COUNTIES.

Belong to the coal formation. All these counties, as may be anticipated from my previous remarks, belong to our bituminous coal formation. In all of them I have seen workable seams of bituminous coal.

Coal on Honey Creek. The principal coal district in Vigo is on Honey creek, between six and seven miles from Terre Haute. The coal here, though superior in geological position, does not lie so high above the water courses as in the previously-described counties, and cannot be worked quite so conveniently on an extensive scale, without sinking shafts. On Section 16, Township 11 N., Range 8 W., there is good coal, some four feet thick, overlaid by a foot of shale.

On Section 9, Township 11 N., Range 8 W., a dark limestone is extensively quarried for building the locks on the Cross-cut canal. The bed is from four to five feet thick, and comes out in fine blocks. It is more durable than the generality of the dark limestones of our coal formation, and answers tolerably well for the purposes to which it has been applied. It is generally thought necessary to make the "coping" of a more permanently durable material; for which purpose the Putnamville rock is usually selected. Dark limestone on Honey creek.

Resting on this limestone is a stratum of shale about one foot thick; and over this is a three-feet bed of slaty sandstone.

A four-feet seam of coal probably lies beneath this limestone.

A slaty and crumbling sandstone exists here in the ridges. The excavations at the summit level of the Cross-cut canal have penetrated some three or four feet into it. Slaty sandstone in the ridges between Honey creek and Eel river.

In Sullivan county I found excellent coal on the head waters of Busseron creek. Here, as on Honey creek, the coal lies rather low to be conveniently worked without sinking shafts. Coal on Busseron.

On Section 5, Township 9 N., Range 8 W., coal has been dug into four feet, and the seam is supposed to be five or six feet thick. The quality of this coal is fair. It is overlaid by slaty sandstone and ferruginous limestone. Above these there appears to be another seam of coal, but it is not well exposed. The best coal which I noticed on Busseron was on the Lick fork, on Section 8, Township 9 N., Range 8 W. Best coal on Lick fork of Busseron creek.

The rock visible in Knox county is chiefly sandstone, some of which may be used for building.

The principal seams of coal from which this county has to look for her supply of this article of fuel, lie on White river. At Edwardsport, at Piersville, at the Uplaw Ford, above the mouth of Prairie creek, and near the junction of the east and west forks, are the most important beds. The only one of these which I have Coal on White river.

yet had an opportunity of examining, is the bed at the Uplaw ford. Here the coal is entirely below low water in White river, and therefore can only be procured in a low stage of water, and even then with inconvenience. In order to work this coal to advantage, it would be necessary to sink a shaft. Its thickness is not known: it has been dug into some two feet.

Sulphuret of zinc.

Above low-water mark at the Upland Ford, is a slaty sandstone, containing some small nodules of carbonate of iron. In breaking some of these, I observed in the center portions of sulpheret of zinc.

White river flows here for about half a mile over coal. I have been told that the coal is more conveniently situated at some of the other coal banks.

One or two thin seams of coal show themselves on White river at low water, below the crossing of the Vincennes and Princeton road.

On Aikman's creek, in Daviess county, on Section 17, Township 2 N., Range 6 W., there is a bed of good coal, the thickness of which has not yet been ascertained. It is overlaid by shale. At Mr. Jet's, some distance off, is a seam, probably the same as the one on Section 17, which is supposed to be six feet thick. In several other places in this neighborhood good coal is visible in the banks of the creeks.

On Section 21, Township 2 N., Range 8 W., there is a fine bed of grey limestone. This rock might be useful in the construction of the New Albany and Vincennes turnpike, both for a building stone and for metaling. It lies only four miles south of the road, and I am told that the engineers, not being aware of the existence of the above locality, had calculated upon having to transport the materials for these purposes, twenty miles.

I picked up some good specimens of iron ore close to this limestone; but have not yet discovered any body of it.

Thick bed of coal on the Patoka.

On the Patoka, in Pike county, within half a mile of the common boundary line between this county and Gibson, on the west half of the north-east quarter of

Section 4, Township 2 S., range 8 W., there is a thick bed of tolerable coal. It is ten feet from the top to the lowest point where an observation can be effected; and it extends beneath this, under water, how far is not known. Over it is a slaty sandstone. In the middle of the coal I observed a stratum of shale, six inches or a foot thick; so that the coal can only be considered about nine feet thick as far as it can be viewed. This and the seam on Brouillet's creek, in Vermillion county, are the two thickest beds of coal I have yet seen in Indiana.

Lower down on the Patoka, I have not yet observed any out croppings of coal.

The lumps of cinder, burnt sandstone, and ferruginous slag, lying in the bed of the Patoka, near the coal bank, seem to indicate that this coal has at some time, been on fire.

On Section 9, Township 25, Range 8 W., I met with a thick bed of grey limestone, covered by sandstone; the same stratum runs some distance into Gibson county.

Some of the sandstones on the Patoka, in Gibson county, afford a pretty good building rock. The abutments of the bridge over the Patoka, on the Vincennes and Princeton road, are built of sandstone quarried on the Patoka three miles above Columbia, on Mr. Townsend's land. Most of it is tolerably free from mica and oxide of iron; and will, therefore, I think, stand well.

COMPARISON BETWEEN THE MURIATIFEROUS ROCKS OF VIRGINIA AND OHIO, AND THOSE AT THE BASE OF THE COAL FORMATION OF INDIANA.

Geology may be truly called a science of analogy. It was a comparison of observations made at distant points, that first drew the attention of the man of science to the striking points of resemblance between certain rocks; and which at length led to the construction of a system, which developed a multitude of important practical facts and principles of the highest interest to mankind.

Our country being a new one, and therefore affording little opportunity, by excavations or borings, to judge of the probability of the existence of salt in its geological formations, I considered that no better means could be adopted for arriving at correct conclusions on so important a point, than a close comparison between the strata in Indiana, which from their geological position were the most likely to afford productive brine, and those older regions of the western country which had been proved by actual borings to be richest in this valuable mineral production. The better to accomplish this object, I took, this summer, a trip to the celebrated salt region of Virginia, on the Kanawha river; and from personal observation, which in all cases is much more satisfactory than written descriptions, however accurate, derived my conclusions regarding the correspondence of the two formations.

The result of these comparative observations has convinced me that the formation which exists in Indiana, in the counties of Warren, Fountain, Parke, Clay, Greene, Martin, Dubois, Perry, and part of Crawford, Orange, Lawrence, Owen and Putnam, is the equivalent of that on the Kanawha and Muskingum, with some difference in the details of their geological features.

They both lie within and near the termination of a bituminous coal formation, and form the base or inferior members of their respective coal measures.

In both, the lowest of these rocks are sandstones of a white or reddish-white color, containing cavities, with beds of coal, shale, and argillaceous rocks overlying them.

In both, the country is elevated into high ridges, with narrow intervening valleys; although, in Indiana, especially in the northern counties, these ridges are not nearly so high as on the Kanawha.

In both, the shales and sandstones alternating with the coal overlying these white sandstones, contain fossil plants; namely, *catamites* (arborescent *equisitated* or horse-tails,) *ferns*, and various species of *Stigmaria* and *Lessidodenron*, *Sigillaria*, *Trigona-carpum*, *Cardio-çarpon* and *Carpolithes*.

On the other hand, in our State I have not yet discovered any conspicuous stratum corresponding either to the "black siliceous slate" of the Kanawha region or the "calcareo-siliceous rock" of the Muskingum salines, described by Dr. Hildreth as a uniform accompaniment of the saliferous rocks of these regions.

Moreover, the red marls, or rather variegated shales, said to be a uniform accompaniment of the muriatiferous strata of the western country, though prevalent in some parts of this section of Indiana, are not so conspicuous as in the corresponding formations of our neighboring States.

In both regions of country, "licks" are of very common occurrence; but I believe that, in some instances, in Indiana, the animals are attracted to these spots, not in consequence of the existence of common salt contained in the soil or springs, as the tests used frequently indicated no appreciable amount; but from the fact of these supposed salt licks holding in solution sulphate of iron (copperas.) Since all kinds of stock in the interior of the American Continent have a great predilection for saline substances generally, this also satisfies that craving.

A few springs impregnated with common salt are to be found in this part of Indiana, as in the equivalent formation of Virginia and Ohio; but they are not so common in our State as might be supposed from the representations of its inhabitants, because many of the mineral springs generally believed to contain salt, have been proved, by the application of nitrate of silver, (solution of lunar caustic)—the decisive chemical test for all chlorides or muriates, either to be destitute of this ingredient, or to contain only a trace.

The evolution of carburetted hydrogen (coal gas,) and the flowing of petroleum, which form in Virginia remarkable burning springs, do not appear to be equally common in the part of Indiana now under consideration.

Upon the whole, therefore, it would seem, though there are some shades of difference between the equivalent formations of the three States; yet that the correspondence is sufficiently close to induce the belief that *there is a tolerably fair prospect that the formation at the margin of the coal fields of Indiana will yield a profitable brine.*

Since making these comparative observations, I have visited a region on Coal creek, in Fountain county, and learned, for the first time, that borings have been effected by Mr. Thomas to the depth of 700 feet, and am therefore enabled to add some interesting facts in corroboration of my previous assumptions, drawn from analogy and from correspondence of geological position.

These borings have been commenced in sandstone rocks, containing specks and veins of carbonaceous matter. At 66 feet 9 inches, a seam of coal was passed through, supposed to be from nine to ten feet thick, covered by a thin seam of shale. The next 120 feet were through sandstone, similar to that above the coal. Then the sandstone rock became whiter and harder; and, after boring ten feet further, or 209 feet 6 inches from the surface, the first vein of salt was reached, but the brine was weak. It was supposed that hereabouts a thin bed of coal was struck. Below this, the rock was still sandstone, but of a bluer color, and continued so to the depth of 300 feet from the surface, excepting very hard vein some 250 feet from the surface, which was thought by Mr. Thomas to be of the nature of flint. At 300 feet the sandstone rock became harder, coarser and whiter, and continued so for 400 feet, making the depth of the borings, in all, 700 feet.

If the reports of these borings be correct, then the succession in Fountain county, near the Wabash river, is as follows, including in this, rocks exposed above the surface on the banks of the Wabash near its confluence with Coal creek:

Section obtained from borings for salt.

1. Soil and subsoil.
2. Drift deposits.
3. Argillaceous shale.
4. Coal, 18 inches to 2 feet.
5. Sandstone, 6 to 8 feet.
6. Thale and good coal, 1½ to 2 feet.
7. Underclay, 8 to 10 feet.
8. Coal, 1½ to 1.5 feet.
9. Underclay, shale, thin coal and sandstone, 10 to 13 feet.
10. Good coal, 1.5 feet.
11. Underclay and shale, 8 feet.
12. Slaty clay with argillaceous iron ore; bands of ore 3 to 4 inches thick.
13. Good coal, 20 inches to 2 feet.
14. Underclay (good fire clay?) white above, dark beneath, 8 feet.
15. Hard bituminous limestone, 5 to 6 feet.
16. Coal, 4.5.
17. Sandstone with specks and veins of carbanaceous matter, intermixed with some shaly layers, 60 to 70 feet.
18. Thin shale, .5 feet.
19. Coal, 9 to 10^2 feet.
20. Sandstone similar to No. 17, 130 feet. Thin coal?
21. White hard sandstone, in which the salt water was first struck, at 209 feet from the surface,—thickness, 36 feet.
22. Hard (chert?) seam.*
23. White and grey sandstone, 54 feet.
24. Coarse, hard, white sandstone, 400 feet.

The white sandstone, the last member of this section, corresponds to the sub-division of the carboniferous

* This might possibly be the equivalent of the "silicious slate," or the "calcareo-siliceous rock" of Dr. Hildreth. The thickness of [illegible] liceous vein was very inconsiderable, some 6 to 12 inches.

rocks known in Great Britain under the name of the Mill-Stone Grit, which comes in between the coal measures and the sub-carboniferous limestones beneath.

It is the very same kind of rock and occupies the same geological horizon as the salt bearing sandstones in which the brines have been obtained, both on the Kanawha, in Virginia; on the Muskingum, in Ohio, and on the Saline, in Illinois.

After reaching the first vein of salt water in Fountain county, in member No. 21 of the preceding section, the auger, in passing through the lower beds, would frequently drop into cavities, from which salt brine issued, in more abundance and stronger as the borings were carried further into Nos. 22, 23 and 24. Such cavities, containing salt, are characteristic of the salt-bearing sandstones at the base of the coal measures at almost all localities where successful borings for salt water have been conducted through our western coal measures. Although the salt water continued very gradually to increase in strength as the borings proceeded, it was not until the spring of 1838, when the last hundred feet were completed, that a strong brine was reached. At present it is said to yield about one bushel of salt from fifty gallons, or one pound to the gallon.* A qualitative analysis of the water, made at the wells, gave the following results:

Acids—

Muriatic,
Sulphuric—a trace,
Carbonic.

Bases—

Soda,
Lime,
Magnesia,
Iron (oxide)—a mere trace.

---

* If it is so, it must be stronger than the average of the Kanawha brine.

If we suppose the acids and bases combined in solution so as to form all the possible soluble salts, we should then have in solution,

Muriate of soda (common salt)—strong.
Muriate of magnesia } (bittern) very small quantity.
Muriate of lime }
Muriate of iron—a mere trace.
Sulphate of soda (Glauber salts)—a mere trace.
Sulphate of magnesia (Epsom salts), do
Sulphate of iron. do
Carbonate of soda.
Bi-carbonate of lime.
Bi-carbonate of iron—a mere trace.*

Judging of the quantities by the appearance of the precipitates, compared with those produced by the Kanawha brine, I should say that there was less bi-carbonate of iron, more bi-carbonate of lime, and less magnesia in the Coal creek, than in the Kanawha brine; if so, it is upon the whole a purer and more valuable brine.

The salt produced is remarkably white, and crystallizes in beautiful cuboidal forms; and those who have tried it, inform me that they prefer it to any other salt for preserving meat.

Another well has been bored by Mr. Wallace, about a quarter or half a mile further up the creek. He has reached the depth of 600 feet, but has not yet obtained as strong a brine as Mr. Thomas procured at 700 feet. The strata passed through are the same as at the other well.

The superposition of the strata immediately above the borings, and lying in the adjoining ridges is nearly the same as represented in the section given in a former

---

* In the absence of a sufficient supply of the salt water, and also for want of time, the quantitative analysis of this salt water has not yet been made.

part of this report, above the mouth of Coal creek, in the same county, only a mile or two from the salt well.

Highly important inferences are to be drawn from these facts, both for the science of Geology, in confirmation of the uniformity of her laws, and in proving the correctness of analogical deductions, founded upon the general principles of the science; but also to Indiana, in developing facts, which before were only probabilities.

Here is demonstrated that the white, cellular sandstones lying toward the boundary and base of our coal formation, are in Indiana, as in Virginia and Ohio, charged with saline matter, and evidently situated here under the same circumstances as in the sister States. This is shown both from the succession of the strata passed through by the auger, the frequent cavities in the rock, the deph at which the saliferous rocks lie, and from the fact, that the brine rises and falls in the well with the change of level of the water in the creek, just as we find it on the Kanawha and Muskingum.

The only doubt remaining as to the ultimate success of the proprietors on Coal creek, is as respects the supply of water. Most of the productive salt works are on the borders of considerable streams. Coal creek, it is true, is not a very large stream; but it runs in the same direction as the dip of the rocks; and the works being but a mile or a mile and a half east of the Wabash river, it is not improbable but that this stream may contribute, by the percolation of its waters through the porus sandrock, to replenish the consumption of water. Mr. Thomas, who has been engaged in the salt business for many years at the Kanawha salines, confidently hopes, from the number and capacity of the cavities passed through, and from the present rise of the brine in the well, that the supply of salt water will be abundant.

If the perseverance of Mr. Thomas and Mr. Wallace be crowned with success, as we do most sincerely hope it may be, then the natural and important inference will be, that, under similar circumstances, the extension of this same formation, which runs in a band from the Ohio to the Wabash, in a course varying from north to north-west, will also yield a productive brine; and if so, Indiana will be rendered entirely independent of other markets for a supply of this indispensable article of consumption.

It should be observed here, that though in Ohio, the most productive salt wells have been bored in strata similar to those just described, and lying in that State above a conglomerate rock and below a silicio-calcareous rock, yet that there is salt in small quantities in lower geological positions, as, for instance, in the Waverly rock, in the black argillaceous slate, and in the underlying calcareous deposits, as also in strata situated above the calcareo-siliceous rock; but none of these formations have afforded as strong a brine as those situated in these intermediate strata. Hence the inference, *that borings for brine east of the second principal meridian, may yield salt water, but are not likely to afford as strong a brine as those west of that line, carried through the white sandstones lying at the margin of our coal basin.*

COMPARISON BETWEEN THE GEOLOGICAL FORMATIONS OF INDIANA AND THOSE OF OHIO.

A study of the reports of the Geology of Ohio, together with some personal observations, have convinced me that there exists a striking analogy between the geological formations of that State and those of Indiana.

The blue fossiliferous limestone has formed, near the common boundary line, a kind of back-bone, which, dipping gently in opposite directions, namely east in Ohio and west in Indiana, gradually disappear, in both States, beneath a series of overlapping strata, which, with one single exception, have a uniform, corresponding character.

The first group which succeeds and overlaps the blue fossiliferous limestones is the series which has been called by Dr. Locke, of Ohio, the cliff rock, comprising the magnesian limestones of upper Silurian date and the coral limestone of Devonian date, of this report. They have been observed in both States, and correspond in superposition, organic remains, and generally in mineralogical structure. They form very frequently, in both States, the falls of the rivers and projecting cliffs, hence Dr. Lockes' name.

In Ohio, they are quarried at Eaton for building rock; in Indiana, they are procured for the same purpose in the hills behind Madison, and extend thence in a northerly curved belt through the State.

On the Ohio river they are visible above the water courses for about twenty or thirty miles. On the Upper Wabash they extend from near the Ohio line to Delphi, more than double that distance, but lie much lower than on the Ohio.

Next in order follows the black argillaceous slate, which in both States laps, and is superincumbent on the coral limestone. In Ohio this deposit forms "the base of the hills capped with sandstone bordering on the Scioto Valley; in Indiana, it extends through the base of the knobs."

The Waverly sandstone rock of the Ohio geologists, which "caps the hills bordering on the Scioto Valley," is the equivalent of the soft, fine-grained, greyish or brownish-grey sandstone of our knobs, running from Floyd county, on the Ohio river, at first north and then north-west, crossing White river at the bluffs below Port Royal.

"Resting on this last described series, occurs," in Ohio as well as Indiana, "a conglomerate." In Indiana, however, this rock is not as rich in pebbles as in Ohio.

In Indiana we have to the west the sub-carboniferous limestone superimposed on the knob freestone; but, judging from the Ohio reports, the sub-carboniferous limestone is absent in that State, and the Scioto freestone- equivalent to our knob-freestone—rests on the conglomerate, or mill-stone grit.

To the sub-carboniferous limestone of Indiana succeeds the conglomerate with the productive coal measures superimposed on it. In Ohio the conglomerate is also the base of her coal measures. The absence of the sub-carboniferous limestone appears, therefore, so far as the Geology of the two States is at present known, to be the principal difference in the geological features of these neighboring States.

Thus, by reversing the dip of the rocks—that of Indiana being westerly, that in Ohio easterly, we have, with the above single exception, the same details of geological formations.

SUMMARY OF THE GEOLOGY OF INDIANA.

During the Geological survey in which I have been engaged for the last two years, I have visited all the counties south of the Wabash, except Adams and Jay, and nearly all the old counties north of this river; indeed, no county has been omitted in my researches, which, from its position, demanded an examination, in order to obtain a clear and correct outline of the geological features and mineral resources of our State.

General features of the Geology of the whole of Indiana ascertained.

Analytical investigations in the laboratory being added to my examinations in the field, it has as yet, of course, been out of my power to carry my observations sufficiently into minutiæ, to enable me to lay down the precise boundary lines of our geological formations in all their meanderings, or to examine every locality which promised to afford valuable minerals; still, with the general course of these lines and the most important mineral localities, I have rendered myself familiar.

As I may not have another opportunity of submitting any further observations for your consideration, I shall now endeavor, before closing this report, to sum up shortly the most important discoveries which have been disclosed by the geological survey in which I have been engaged, and to draw various useful and practical inferences therefrom.

Our bituminous coal formation part of a great basin.

Our bituminous coal formation is part of a great coal-field, which includes, besides almost the whole of sixteen counties, and part of nine counties, in Indiana, nearly the whole of lower Illinois, and eight or ten counties in the north-western part of Kentucky.

Area of coal formation.

This bituminous coal formation occupies, in Indiana, an area of about 7,524 square miles, and includes all the counties lying west of the following described line:

General eastern boundary line of coal formation.

Commencing on the Ohio, where the second principal meridian crosses that river; this line runs first north-west, crosses the base line near the middle of Range 2 west; thence, nearly north, crosses the east fork of White river, two or three miles east of the line between Martin and Lawrence; thence north-west by north up Indian creek, to a point two or three miles west of the north-east corner of Green county; thence north-west to Mill creek in Owen county; crosses this creek one or two miles below the Falls; thence nearly north to the National road; crosses this road one or two miles west of Putnamville; thence north-west to the south-west corner of Montgomery county; thence nearly north along the line between this county and Fountain; crosses the Upper Wabash near Independence; thence, mostly concealed by drift deposits, to a point near where the south line of land district No. 7 intersects the Illinois boundary line in Jasper county and about six miles to where the Iroquois river crosses the boundary line between Indiana and Illinois, into which last State the continuation of said line runs, preserving nearly the same north-west curve, near the forks of the Illinois river, below Ottawa; and thence to near the Grand Rapids, and mouth of Rock river.

Outliers of coal beyond this line.

Such is the *general* boundary of the coal field of Indiana, although some outliers of this formation extend some distance beyond this line.

Montgomery and Tippecanoe counties not in coal formation.

The northern extension of this line, after crossing the National Road, inclines more to the west than I formerly conjectured, and therefore excludes nearly the whole of Montgomery and Tippecanoe counties from the coal region; a part of which counties I supposed contained within it, when I penned my last report.

The counties entirely included within the coal formation, are, therefore: Posey, Vanderburgh, Warrick, Spencer, Dubois, Pike, Gibson, Knox, Daviess, Martin, Sullivan, Clay, Vigo, Parke, Vermillion and Fountain; also the greatest part of Warren, Greene and Perry, lies within it, and the south-west portion of Jasper and Owen, besides small strips of the western parts of Putnam, Lawrence, Orange and Crawford.

Counties included in coal formation.

The accompanying map* will show, at a glance, the extent of the coal formation: that part of the State is colored brown (burnt sienna).

The belt colored with indigo blue, immediately east of said boundary line, represents, approximately, the area occupied by the sub-carboniferous limestone.

Zone of subcarboniferous limestoue.

The wider zone east of the sub-carboniferous limestone, colored light yellow, indicates the approximate area of the knob-freestone, including, however, the subordinate intercalated beds of encrinital limestones and grey argillaceous shales.

Zone of knob stones.

The narrow zone, tinted with India ink, shows the area of the black bituminous slate running through the base of the knobs.

Zone of black slate.

The light Prussian blue tint east of this black slate, indicates the coral limestone of the Falls of the Ohio.

Zone of coral limestone.

The darker tint of the same denotes the magnesian limestones of upper Silurian date.

Zone of magnesian limestone.

The darkest tint of the same on the extreme east, marks the area of the blue limestone, marlites and subordinate beds of fine siliceous mudstones of lower silurian date, embracing the most easterly counties bordering on the State of Ohio.

Zone of blue limestone.

All of these rock formations are covered to a great extent by drift, that is, by beds of sand, clay, and gravels, in which large masses of granite and other crystal-

Extent of drift.

* The original geological map, here referred to, was deposited in the State library, but has not been published.

ine rocks, called bowlders, or lost rocks, are numerous. This drift is more extensive north of the National Road, than south of it.

Some bowlders in coal formation.

Bowlders are most common over the northern extension of the sub-carboniferous formation, they are, however, occasionally met with over the coal formation.

Best beds of coal near the eastern boundary line.

The best seams of coal observed are those which crop out, or come to the surface, some eight or ten miles from the boundary line. The best coal which I have yet seen in the State, is near the Sugar creek Foundry, in Parke county. The two thickest seams yet observed, are on the Patoka, between Pike and Gibson counties, and on Brouillet's creek, in Vermillion county.

The eastern out-croppings, though originally the lower beds, lie now higher above the water-courses than those in the south-west counties.

Coal can be worked by open drifts.

Some of these coals can be worked by open drifts, above the drainage of the country; others by sinking shafts, as in Great Britain; but instead of going, as is frequently the case in that country, to the depth of several thousand feet, it is probable that most of the workable coals in Indiana can be reached by shafts put down in proper situations, at from 50 to 500 feet, or less, from the surface.

Vegetable structure of coal in Indiana.

The bituminous coal of Indiana shows its vegetable origin more distinctly than any other coal I ever inspected. Spots and even regular layers of absolute charcoal, from which the woody fibre can be distinctly detached, are frequent in the superior beds of this country.

Coal measures not much disturbed.

Although faults, or dislocations of a few inches, are occasionally visible in our coal fields, no important slips, and no veins of trap, basalt, or greenstone, so common in those of North Britain, have been therein observed. This indicates that our coal strata are not much disturbed, at least near the surface; a considerable advantage, as it enables the miner readily to trace each particular vein. If our coal-beds be divided by faults into a number of water-tight compartments, the water can be conveniently pumped out of them by the aid of a steam-engine; but if the water communication be continuous, it would add, of course, to the expense of mining; to ascertain this is, therefore, one of the objects to be obtained by a closer geological examination of our coal formation than there has yet been time and opportunity to make.

Dip of the rocks.

The general dip of the rocks is very gradual toward the west, or centre of the basin, except where they undulate. The precise dip has not yet been ascertained.

The deposits of hydrated brown oxide of iron, which occur amongst the coal sandstones, are for the most part too impure to be worked with profit.

Argillaceous iron ore and carbonate of iron in coal formation.

Localities demanding the inspection of iron-masters.

Large quantities of argillaceous iron ore and carbonate of iron lie, associated with the slaty clays of our coal formation, particularly along its eastern margin. Those which I have seen particularly worthy the attention of iron masters wishing to settle in the West, are situated on Brouillet's creek, in Vermillion county; on the Wabash and Coal creek, in Fountain county; on Sugar and Racoon creeks, in Parke county; on Eel river and White river, in Clay and Greene counties; on Anderson creek, in Perry county; and on Pine, in Warren county.

Clays, hearth-stones, copperas & alum in coal formation.

Along the margin of our coal formation, I find excellent fire-clays, potter's clay, furnace hearth-stones, and slates, from which copperas and alum can be manufactured on a large scale.

Sandstone at margin of coal formation often valuable for minerals.

The sandstones at the base of the coal formation, afford, upon the whole, the best freestones for construction; but there are other freestones interstratified between the coal beds, that can be used also advantageously for the same purpose. They have been, hitherto, too much overlooked by engineers. I am in hopes that, for beauty, durability, and the ease with which they can be worked, the white and fine-grained of these rocks will prove to be superior, for architectural purposes, to many limestones generally preferred. The most splendid buildings in the New Town of Edinburgh and in Glasgow, in Scotland, are constructed of a white, small-grained, siliceous sandstone, procured from an analogous formation in that country. Melrose Abbey, which is seven hundred years old, is built of the same material, and the "cornices are still as sharp and perfect as if they had been carved only a few years ago."

Rock of this character has come under my notice, particularly in Warren, Fountain and Orange counties; but it is probable that most of the intermediate counties, lying as they do in the corresponding line of formation, will be found to yield a similar material.

Prospect of discovering salt.

The prospect of the discovery of profitable salt water, by boring, in favorable situations, through the white sandstones at the margin of the coal formation, is very favorable. These rocks are evidently charged with common salt, and are the equivalent of the well-known saliferous formation on the Kanawha and Muskingum. A brine affording a pound of salt from a gallon of water has been procured from this formation, near the mouth of Coal creek, in Fountain county.

The large streams of Indiana run in a direction corresponding nearly with the dip of our coal measures. This is considered favorable for the retention and rise of salt water, in situations where, as in our saliferous formation, the streams seem to afford the supply of water which feeds our salt springs. We may, therefore, flatter ourselves that, before long, the enterprise of our citizens will produce salt sufficient to render us entirely independent of other states for this indispensable article of consumption, and to furnish, probably, a supply for exportation.

Limestones are not abundant in our coal formation. They are locally present and often afford good materials for constructions, and macadamizing our turnpikes. Most of the limestones in the coal measurers are dark colored. The darkest of these, especially when they contain argillaceous or clayey matter, are liable to crack with the action of the sun and frost; but some of them are durable and hard enough to take a polish, affording a black marble of considerable beauty.

Chemical analysis will greatly aid in deciding on the comparative value of these limestones, freestones, coals, iron ores, hydraulic limestones, potters' clays, saline materials, &c.

Limestones seem to be more abundant in the upper coal measures than in the middle or lower members. **Limestones more abundant, &c.**

The margin of our coal formation is elevated into much higher ridges than the interior portion of it; the country therefore, is generally more broken here than nearer the Wabash river. **Country broken near boundary of coal formation.**

Sand predominates in the soils of this region, evidently because sandstones are the most abundant and thickest portion of the coal measures. **Sand predominates in soils over the coal formation.**

We have reason to congratulate ourselves, that so large a portion of our State is occupied by the coal formation, when we consider that on this mineral is based the enterprise and industry of most of the great manufacturing districts of Great Britain. In alluding to this formation, Dr. Thompson, the celebrated Scotch chemist, makes the following pertinent remarks:

"The coal measures constitute the great source of the industry and wealth of Great Britain. All the manufacturing districts, with a few exceptions, which admit of an easy explanation, are situated in the immediate vicinity of coal. Bristol, Coventry, Birmingham, Swansen, Wolverhampton, the Potteries, Nottingham, Sheffield, Manchester, Halifax, Leeds, Huddersfield, Newcastle, are all situated in coal districts." **Coal measure great source of wealth in Great Britain**

I am confirmed in the correctness of the opinion expressed in my report of last year:—"*that no perfect workable seams of bituminous coal alternate with any of the members of the sub-carboniferous formation.*" It would, therefore, be useless to search for bituminous coal beneath the light-colored limestones of Harrison, Crawford, Orange, Lawrence, Monroe, Owen and Putnam counties, or amongst any of the strata in any of the counties east of these. **No perfect seams of coal in sub-carboniferous formation.**

Judging from analogy, borings for salt commenced beneath these limestones, though they might reach good **Salt water procured in strata beneath mill-**

stone grit formation, generally weak. salt water, would, probably, not afford a supply that could compete with the brines procured from the base of the coal formation.

Oolitic limestones how known. The limestone formation, the termination of the true carboniferous and saliferous rocks, is distinguished by the two characteristic fossils,—the *Pentremite* and *Archimedes*, and by the oölitic structure (grain like the roe of a fish) which some of its members possess.

Good building rock. This limestone series affords, in the above counties, good building materials, and a cream-colored marble from the oölitic members. The oölitic limestone makes

White lime. the whitest and most valuable lime of any rock at present observed in the West.

Prospects for lead ore in sub-carboniferous limestone. Since the sub-carboniferous limestones of Illinois, as well as the magnesian limestone of upper Silurian date of Wisconsin and Iowa, afford ores of lead, there is reason to believe that the corresponding formations in Indiana might yield similar ores. The galena of the sub-carboniferous limestone of Southern Illinois is associated with fluor spar (fluate of lime,) which is there, in fact, the vein stone of that ore. This will serve as an excellent guide for the discovery of galena, if it should exist in Indiana under the same circumstances. No important vein has yet been discovered; but a more detailed survey might lead to discoveries of veins.

Resting on the upper beds of the sub-carboniferous limestone and between them and the lower members of the coal measures and mill stone grit, are some rich

Beds of iron ore over oolitic limestone series. beds of hydrated brown oxide of iron. The most important are those in the neighborhood of Mill creek and Eel river, in Putnam and Owen counties.

Formation in Indiana corresponding to the iron region in Tennessee. The soft freestones, limestones, porous silicious rocks and ferruginous clays, extending through the counties of Floyd, Washington, Jackson, and the eastern part of Morgan, Monroe and Harrison, are analogous to the well known iron regions on the Cumberland river, which has yielded large amounts of hydrated brown oxide of iron, and kept in blast so many furnaces. In Tennessee, this ore has generally been discovered in ferruginous clays, resting on limestones, with isolated masses of white siliceous rocks imbedded in it. In this part of Indiana, I have not yet discovered any important beds of iron ore similarly situated; but in the argillaceous beds beneath, extending through the knobs, argillaceous iron ore and carbonate of iron have been discovered in considerable quantities. This ferruginous deposit is well worthy the attention of iron masters.

The soft freestone of the knobs is the equivalent of the rock which "caps the hills bordering on the Scioto valley,"—the Waverly rock of the Ohio Geologists,—which, by judicious selection, affords excellent freestones for building. **Soft freestone knobs equivalent to Waverly rock of Ohio.**

The black slate in the base of these knobs is the equivalent of the Scioto slates and shales.

This black argillaceous deposit has been bored through in Floyd county, and the result has fully proved the fact, *that no perfect seams of coal are associated with it.* **No perfect coal with this slate.**

This formation will yield locally both copperas and alum, by the process described in the body of the report.

Hydraulic limestone, building-stone, lime and mineral manure are the most important materials observed amongst the coral limestones of Devonian date. **Hydraulic limestones & building stones.**

The magnesian limestones of the underlying limestone group of upper Silurian date, are durable rocks for constructions. Hydraulic limestones also occur towards the base of this group, and burr mill-stones are likewise found locally amongst the upper members of this group.

The oldest and originally deepest seated of the rocks of Indiana are the blue fossiliferous limestones, alternating with clays, marls and marlite, and fine grained siliceous mudstones, in Switzerland, Dearborn, Union, and the eastern part of Fayette, Franklin, Ripley and Jefferson counties. **Blue fossiliferous limestones.**

These limestones, though not generally in as thick strata as the previously described superincumbent magnesian limestones, are suitable for building, and some **Building rock**

Marble procured from them.

of the beds are susceptible of receiving a good polish, and produce a marble of a variegated appearance.

Shell marble of Jefferson county.

The murchisonia shell limestone of Jefferson county is the best building stone found in this formation. This rock makes also a beautiful marble, perhaps the most beautiful of any rock in the State.

Clays rather fusible.

Marls valuable.

The clays generally contain a percentage of lime, which renders them rather fusible. The marls would be very valuable for improving some of the sandy soils of the western counties. When this country becomes older and produce more valuable, these marls could be transported by water with great advantage, from Jefferson, Switzerland and Dearborn, to the counties on the Ohio and Wabash, which are deficient in lime, phosphoric acid, potash and clayey matter. This will, undoubtedly, some day be done.

Rich in fossils

Most of the lowest beds are vastly rich in fossils, a list and drawings of which can be furnished for publication, if required. They correspond generally with those of the lower Silurian rocks of Great Britain and the eastern continent, and the Hudson river group and Trenton limestone of New York.

Flatness of the ridge dividing the waters of the Gulf of St. Lawrence and those of the Gulf of Mexico.

It is a remarkable feature in the physical geography of our northern counties, that a nearly flat prairie country should form the dividing ridges between the waters flowing into the Gulf of St. Lawrence and those running in the Gulf of Mexico; and that our large streams, instead of commencing by confined mountain torrents, should rise from widely expanded sluggish springs in Tamarack swamps, and flow for thirty or forty miles with little perceptible fall.

It is stated, by Jean Baptist Richardville, chief of the Miami nation, that, during a very wet time, the Indians have floated canoes from the waters of the Wabash into the Lakes, and the past wet season has almost proved the possibility of such an undertaking.*

* There are many reasons for believing that the St. Joseph and St. Mary's once flowed down the Wabash. Little river runs now in a nar-

Such being the state of things in the north, it must, of course, be highly favorable for the formation of bog-iron ore, if the copious springs, which are highly charged with carbonic acid, should flow over deep-seated beds of iron ore. The number of chalybeate springs seems to render this highly probable. Northern counties favorable for the formation of bog iron.

Several localities which afford this ore have been indicated in the body of this report, besides those mentioned in that of last year. The counties in which there appear to be the greatest indications of bog ore, and which demand more particularly the inspection of iron masters in search of this kind of ore, are, St. Joseph, Elkhart, La Porte, Pulaski, Fulton, Allen, Huntington, Wabash, Miami, Tippecanoe, Carroll, Randolph, Wayne, Hamilton and Marion; but good localities may probably be discovered in some of the adjoining counties. Localities demanding the attention of iron masters.

On examining the surface and sub-soils in some of the north-east counties, where the fertility was much greater than the external sandy appearance indicated, I discovered that there was a considerable per centage of carbonate of lime in the superior soil, and that it was Cause of fertility of the soil in the north.

---

row channel, some twenty or thirty yards wide, with a very gentle descent, in a flat plain, bounded on both sides by low ridges, uniformly about a mile apart, which bear every appearance of having been the ancient banks of a considerable stream; while the other fork, on the contrary, which joins it below Huntington, now the main branch of the Wabash, shows not the slightest appearance of ever having been much larger than it is at this moment. If we trace Little river to its source, we shall find it issuing from a Tamarack swamp, hardly three miles from the junction of the St. Joseph and St. Mary's. These two rivers rise in Ohio, flow into Indiana in a south-west course, and, when within three miles of the heads of Little river, join, suddenly turn round, and take a nearly opposite course towards the north-east. The St. Joseph now feeds the Wabash and Erie canal, which runs without a single lock for nearly eighteen miles, along the northern bank of the valley through which Little river flows. When we consider all these circumstances, we see at once the probability of the conjecture, that these rivers were once the head waters of the Wabash, and wonder at the insignificant barrier which now turns their course, and at the slight cause which may have wrought so great a change in the destination of their waters.

underlaid by a fatty marl. This accounts, at once, for the productiveness of these lands, and the retentive nature of a soil apparantly nearly pure sand.

Several pieces of native copper have been found, besides those mentioned on a previous occasion. From the nature of the ore and its uniform association with drift or bowlders of crystalline and volcanic rocks, there is little doubt but that this copper ore originates in a distant formation, probably the same from which the primitive debris has been derived.

Bog ore, calcareous tufa, and peat, the only mineral deposits likely to be found in the north.

The extensive drift of the north, and the uniform flatness of the country, render it improbable that any important mineral deposits will ever be discovered here, except bog-iron ore, calcareous tufa and peat.

Geology of Indiana, Ohio, Kentucky and Illinois very analagous.

The leading features in the geology of Indiana, Ohio, Kentucky and Illinois, are very analagous; all are, therefore, likely to afford a similar variety of mineral productions.

The formations of the Cumberland Mountain and Middle Tennessee the same with those of Indiana.

Tennessee embraces a greater variety of geological formations; but its most extensive deposits, the coal measures of the Cumberland mountains, and the limestone series of middle Tennessee, are the equivalents of our carboniferous, sub-carboniferous groups, and underlying black slate and limestones of Devonian and Silurian date, and agree with them in all their essential characters.

Mineral and agricultural resources of Indiana.

Although we may not be able to boast of the gold mines of Georgia and the Carolinas, or of as great a variety of metallic ores as Missouri and Tennessee; yet when we consider the area and probable thickness of our coal measures, with the number of beds of coal, and associate iron ores; their accessibility and proximity to the materials required for their reduction; the levelness, fertility and extent of the arable lands of Indiana; the prospects for an ample supply of salt, and that all these staple articles lie in the immediate vicinity of our principal navigable streams, we have every reason to be abundantly satisfied, not only with our agricultural advantages, but also with our mineral resources, which are, in fact, far greater than could reasonably be anticipated, considering our position near the center of the vast and fertile Valley of the Mississippi. Looking to the sources of wealth and the stimulants to industry which lie buried in the strata of our coal formation, we may confidently anticipate that our young and growing State will not only continue to rival her sister States as an agricultural people, but that she will also, ere long, be able to enjoy an equal share in all their commercial and manufacturing advantages.

Margin of the coal formation the mineral region of the State.

In conclusion I would remark, as the result of my geological examinations in Indiana, that I consider the margin of the coal formation the mineral region of the State, and the one which, before all others, demands a minute topographical, geological survey, in order,

1st. To lay down on the map accurately the boundary of the coal formation in all its meanders.

2d. To examine thoroughly the saliferous rocks, and determine their exact thickness, extent, inclination and superposition.

3d. To discover, if possible, new deposits of iron ore, which seem to be so frequent in this region.

4th. To ascertain the extent of the freestones of this district which might be suitable for building.

5th. To ascertain the number, thickness, relative superposition, equivalency and spaces which the various beds occupy relatively to each other, and the localities where each bed crops out on the surface.

6th. To make observations on the exact dip of the coal measures, a discovery of which would indicate the depth at which any particular seam might be reached by shafts sunk in any part of the coal measures.

7th. To endeavor to discover the most valuable beds of fire-clays, potter's clays, grits and alum slates, which appear to be common in these localities.

8th. To collect an determine what may be the most characteristic fossils, not only of each system and formation, but of the different members of each group; an investigation which is intimately connected with the discovery of mineral wealth; especially with the discovery of workable coal beneath the drainage of the country.

9th. To determine in what this formation agrees, and in what it differs from equivalent formations in other countries.

I am now engaged in my laboratory completing some analyses of coals, ores, &c., collected during this season, (1838,) and hope to be able to submit them in an appendix to this report.

APPENDIX.

Quantitative Analysis of the Mineral Water on Big Pigeon creek, near Evansville, Vanderburg county.

Specific gravity, 1.011.

Gases condensed in water (after 30 miles transportation in a sealed stone bottle:)

Carbonic acid gas (choke-damp of miners) 6 cubic inches in a wine gallon.

Light carburetted hydrogen gas (fire-damp) ....2.5 " "

Nitrogen gas (azote)......................3.5 " "

Saline contents in 100 grains of the water:

Muriate of soda (common salt) 1. 5 grains.

Bi-carbonate of iron ....0.43 "

Bi-carbonate of magnesia........0.33 "

Solid contents at well 2.30

Loss by standing:

Carbonate of iron.................................... 0.31

Carbonate of magnesia...................... . 0.21

Carbonic acid 0.24

Deduct for deposit and escape.... .... 0.76

Saline contents after standing... .... 1.54

This gives 2.82 ounces, or 2 ounces 7 drams in a gallon saline contents after standing, of which 2 ounces 2 scruples 8 grains are common salt.

5*

Light carburetted hydrogen gas rises freely, and escapes continually from the water in the well.

Qualitative Analysis of the Mineral Water at the French Lick.

Muriate of soda (common salt,) strong.
Muriate of lime.
Muriate of magnesia.
Sulphate of magnesia, (Epsom salts.)
Sulphate of soda.
Bi-carbonate of lime; and, perhaps, carbonate of soda.

Quantitative Analysis of a Marl from B. C. Macy's land, Posey county.

Moisture	2.0
Carbonate of lime	36.2
Insoluble residuum (chiefly silica and almnina with a little oxide of iron)	60.0
Oxide of iron	0.8
Loss	1.0
	100.0

Quantitative Analysis of the "Vein Ore" from Brouillet's creek, Vermillion county.

(A variety intermediate between the "hematites" or "hydrated brown oxides of iron," and the "argillaceous iron ores.")

Water	10.
Insoluble silicates	30.

Alumina (the pure adhesive earth of clay).....	8.
Protoxide of iron....................................	45.
Sesquioxide of iron..................................	5.
Loss	2.
	100.

The quantity of metallic iron in the ore is 38.4 per cent. It may, therefore, be expected to yield from 35 to 40 per cent. of cast iron in the furnace.

Quantitative Analysis of the Ferruginous Limestone from the same place on which the ore rests.

Carbonate of lime (limestone)	84.0
Insoluble matter—silica, alumina, and a trace of oxide of iron..................................	9.6
Protoxide of iron....................................	3.5
Loss..	2.8
	100.00

This limestone if used as a flux in the iron furnace, would, therefore, yield at the same time 3 or 4 per cent. of iron.

Examination of the Coal from the Sugar creek Foundry, Parke county.

Specific gravity, 1.219.

Volatile matter..................................	52.1
Carbon in coke	43.9
Ashes (white) ....from	3 to 4.0
	100.0

*100 grains of nitrate of potash required 16 grains of this coal for complete decomposition. Calculating

CPSIA information can be obtained
at www.ICGtesting.com
Printed in the USA
LVHW040618020223
738427LV00006B/649

9 783375 142100